COMMANDER IN CHIEF

JA Armstrong

CHAPTER ONE

Candace Reid listened attentively as each person facing her took a turn apprising her of concerns and potential issues across the globe. The occasional glance at a document presented the only evidence of a diversion in her attention. She accepted a folder from NSA Director Joshua Tate. Her eyes held his momentarily before her hands lifted the cover. The room fell silent as she studied the contents without comment. Page by page, she flipped through the information, committing it to memory and filing away questions that she would need to address beyond this meeting and its participants. She closed the cover and peered over the top of her glasses at Director Tate. "How credible is this information?"

"The sources are credible enough that you're holding it," he replied.

Candace nodded her understanding, removed her glasses, and allowed her gaze to meet each person as she spoke. "I understand that this is as far as it goes for the next couple of months. Be aware that when you bring this to me after January, I will expect more than credible enough." She held up her hand to stall any objections. "I don't need to hear your objection to see them. Understand, I will expect to know where the information you place in my hands came from—if not the who, the where. You cannot expect me to make sound judgments without something tangible, and that includes the origin of information."

Tate nodded. "I think we're all clear on that point."

"Good." Candace smiled. "In that case, I look forward to our next meeting." The group stood nearly in unison. Candace shook hands and thanked the group. "Joshua." She held Tate's hand. "Stay for a moment?"

"Ma'am."

Candace directed the NSA director to have a seat when the room had cleared.

"What can I do for you?" Tate inquired.

"I have a few important decisions facing me."

"So, I understand."

Candace chuckled. "Not the best-kept secret."

He smiled. "Not exactly."

Candace was genuinely amused. Cable news had been droning on and on, debating which people should fill Candace's cabinet. She'd found some of the debate entertaining. Lately, she welcomed a few minutes of diversion. Twenty-four-hour days seemed commonplace. Her head might be hitting the pillow at midnight; sleep seemed determined to elude her. Five million details to address and five million more decisions seemed to demand her attention. Filling her cabinet was her paramount concern. That is what had led her to ask the NSA Director to stay behind. While she enjoyed the banter of pundits, and the suppositions of "experts," Candace put stock in those she trusted. One of the names continually raised by people in Candace's inner-circle was Joshua Tate.

"Well," Candace began. "I'm always fascinated by the things people know I am about to say or do."

"I can only imagine."

"You might have heard that I have some positions to fill."

"I seem to vaguely recall that."

Candace chuckled. Good answer. Candace valued the ability of those closest to her to speak openly, to challenge her assumptions, while understanding that her decisions, once she made them were final. "You have a fan base," she told him.

"I hardly think that."

"Mmm. You enjoy the respect of people whom I trust implicitly."

Tate nodded.

"I need someone, Joshua, who can sit across from me and be willing to deliver the news I don't want to hear candidly. I need someone who will answer my questions honestly and directly—someone who isn't afraid to challenge me. Also, the people who work with me must understand that final decisions rest with me. Regardless of where the chips may fall, it will be my responsibility to account for those decisions. I will not pass that responsibility to my staff. Their responsibility will be to provide me with the facts as they understand those facts, and to give me an honest, forthright assessment of what those facts mean." Candace took a breath. "I need someone, Joshua, that I can trust to be candid with me in private. Someone who understands the need to stand shoulder to shoulder with me publicly. We both know what you shared today barely scratches the surface of what this country faces in an ever-changing world." She offered the stoic man a smile. "I'd like you to come on as my National Security Adviser."

Tate stared blankly at the President-elect. He'd briefed the woman several times, and encountered her during her time on Capitol Hill. Tate had been drilled for several hours by Candace's transition team including the incoming Vice President, and had spent nearly four hours with the former Governor of New York answering a line of questions that had astounded him with their insight. He had never expected an offer to come his way.

"You look surprised," Candace observed.

"I am."

"You shouldn't be." Candace left her seat and walked to a cabinet in the corner of the office. "Scotch?"

Tate nodded.

"Neat or on the rocks?"

"However you take it."

Candace's eyes sparkled with amusement. "Neat it is." She handed him a glass and resumed her seat. "You have advocates, Joshua."

"You're referring to Jane," he surmised.

"Not just Jane."

"Alex?"

Candace smiled. "Trust, as I am sure you are aware, is a precious commodity in this line of business. It becomes a rarity at this level."

Tate listened without comment, sipping his scotch as he regarded Candace from over the top of his glass.

"The world is a complicated place," she said. "People are not as complicated."

He smiled.

"People do, however, make the world complicated."

"They do," he agreed.

"I need someone I can count on," Candace said.

Tate nodded. "Other than the endorsements of the former First Lady and Agent Toles, why me?"

"That's not enough?" Candace teased. "Joshua, you have the experience I need. You understand something that too many people do not."

"What's that?"

"That everything that happens in our world in some way will shape everything else that happens." She sipped from her glass and set it aside. "Too often, I've seen leaders commit the cardinal sins of leadership."

"What might those be?"

"For starters, they overestimate themselves and underestimate the concerns and perspectives of those surrounding them. You know as well as I do that how we train our military will impact outcomes. How much we invest in soft power will play a significant role in how we deploy those men and women serving in our military around the globe. Our economy in many ways dictates our bearing in the world. Someone is always seeking to undermine our efforts and agenda. The idea that a foreign policy adviser needs no understanding, experience, and command of domestic problems is outdated at best. You have that experience. You've worked for FINCEN, you've worked in the upper echelons of the FBI, and you've sat in the director's chair at NSA. Who would be more qualified?"

"I don't have the military background," he offered.

"No. I have military advisers." She smiled. "The Joint Chiefs as an example. I will have a Defense Secretary. And, let's be honest, you will have dozens of people bending your ear with that experience."

"I don't know what to say."

"Yes, you do." Candace smiled.

"I'd be honored."

"Good answer," she replied. "Just remember what an absolute bitch I can be."

Tate laughed. Direct, candid, strong-willed, deliberate — all words he would use to describe the incoming president. Bitch would be nowhere on the list.

"May I ask…"

"We'll make a formal announcement this week," she told him. "Thank you for taking one major issue off my plate."

"I hope I can ease more than one."

Candace raised her class as a toast. "So, do I."

⁜

"How's Mom?"

Jameson looked up from the paper in front of her. "Busy."

Marianne took the newspaper from Jameson's hands and laid it on the table. "Feeling lonely?"

Jameson laughed. Lonely? She was hardly lonely. Between the presence of Secret Service agents, the comings and goings of advisers, and the constant calls and visits from family, Jameson wasn't sure she could remember the last time she'd been alone. "I don't think I've been alone longer than it takes me in the shower in the last two weeks."

Marianne nodded. "I don't think being alone and being lonely are the same thing."

"They're not," a voice offered.

Marianne smiled at her mother.

Candace made her way to Jameson and placed a kiss on her cheek.

"Meeting's over?" Jameson guessed.

"It is."

"How did it go?"

"He accepted."

"That's good."

Candace sighed. "Marianne, would you give us a minute?"

Marianne winked at Jameson and left the kitchen.

"I know that look," Jameson said.

"Is that right?"

"Don't you start worrying about me."

Candace took the opportunity to plop down into Jameson's lap. "Who says I'm worried?"

"I'm all right," Jameson promised.

"I know you are."

"You do?"

"Yes, I do. But, I was hoping I might entice you to spend the rest of the evening with me. Unless you'd rather be alone."

Jameson's eyes met Candace's thoughtfully. Two weeks felt like two years, at least, they did to Jameson. If Jameson had thought that life on the campaign trail was a whirlwind, life with the next president was nothing short of a hurricane. People blew in and out everywhere Candace was. There were decisions to be made every second. Jameson understood the situation. Candace had roughly nine weeks to assemble a cabinet and secure her closest advisers. The daily briefings she received were longer than they had ever been as governor or on the campaign trail. She frequently spoke with President Wallace. Amid what Jameson was certain were pressing national security concerns, domestic issues, and policy foibles, Candace also had to deal with the organization of an Inauguration, writing a speech, making appearances on and off, providing input regarding the private living quarters of The White House, and preparing the family for a transition like no other. On top of it, tomorrow was Thanksgiving. Candace and Jameson would be leaving New York on Sunday and taking up residence at the townhouse they owned in Virginia. That decision had been made more for Cooper's benefit. Cooper would be attending a new school. Candace wanted him to adjust as much as possible before they moved into that big white house.

"I know you have a million things to do," Jameson offered.

"True," Candace admitted. "The kids will all be here tomorrow and then..."

"And then the chaos becomes mania?"

Candace grinned. "Something like that." She wrapped her arms around Jameson's neck. "Do you want the truth?"

"Please."

"Marianne is right."

"I'm okay, Candace."

"I know you are," Candace said, surprising Jameson with the assuredness on her voice. "I know," she repeated. "I'm okay too. I've never been one to settle for that—not for long."

Jameson chuckled. True.

"I don't know if you need it, but I need some time with you—Just you. Just you and me without any of the kids or the world looking in."

"What do you suggest?" Jameson asked.

"I sent Dana home. I sent Grant home. Marianne is headed to Scott's in an hour. She offered to have Cooper spend the night there. She'll be here with the kids early tomorrow morning so..."

"So? It's just you and me?"

Candace smiled.

Jameson let out a sigh of relief. "Candace..."

Candace's lips found Jameson's. "I don't want you to worry about what I need to do. What I need is you," Candace said.

"And some Chinese take-out?"

"I wouldn't say no."

Jameson laughed. "I'm sold."

"That quickly?" Candace teased.

"Well, if you want me to go up on my rates..." Jameson's thought was silenced by a kiss. "On second thought."

Candace closed her eyes and let her head fall onto Jameson's shoulder. "Thank you."

Jameson closed her eyes. "How do you feel about a nap?"

"You're already putting me to bed?"

Jameson opened her eyes and grinned. She stood up still holding Candace.

"You are nuts," Candace laughed.

"So, you've said." Jameson carried Candace into the living room and toward the stairs.

"Jameson! Put me down, you lunatic, before you hurt yourself."

Marianne peeked around the corner and rolled her eyes. "I hope the Secret Service isn't opposed to Bible Study." She laughed when she heard her mother's voice again.

"Jameson!"

"Be quiet, Nana," Jameson said.

Marianne rolled her eyes. "God help The White House."

"I want to know what we can expect from this woman."

"She's thorough."

"Unlike Wallace?"

Petru Rusnac shrugged. "She's not Wallace."

"Obviously. What does that mean going forward?"

"The new president is a mystery to all of us."

"I pay you to solve mysteries, not to find them."

"That may be," Rusnac said. "I cannot tell you how deeply connected she is. She shares a close relationship with Jane Merrow."

A furrowed brow raised.

Rusnac sighed. "Yuri," he began cautiously. "It will take time to assess Mrs. Reid."

"We do not have time. This is not a game. We need to move now."

"That might prove unwise without more information."

"Then decode the mystery."

Rusnac nodded. The last person he wanted to cross was Yuri Sokolov. Sokolov had replaced Viktor Ivanov at the helm of Advance Strategic Applications. ASA was a technology company based in Moscow whose business interests extended far beyond the company mission statement. It served as a front for the Russian SVR. Its roots planted at the end of World War II had grown into tentacles stretching across the globe. ASA had invested in Bradley Wolfe's bid for the US presidency in every way imaginable. Its surrogates had waged a disinformation campaign, funneled money to Wolfe's campaign, paid for ads through corporate and diplomatic loopholes, and mustered the support of its allies in the states to discredit Candace Reid. The Governor of New York's ascension to the highest seat of power in the world was less than ideal. She was a known quantity as a legislator. How she would react when presented with intelligence and military options remained a puzzle for nearly everyone. Rusnac's wealth and all that came with it continued at the pleasure of the man seated before him. He had failed in the task he had been given. Now, he needed to prove his worth.

"What is it you want to know?" Rusnac asked.

"Everything."

Candace leaned back into Jameson's embrace and sipped a glass of wine. Jameson had built a fire and ordered Chinese take-out as promised. It was the perfect evening. Candace would miss her time in Schoharie. It was her haven; the place she felt the most at ease.

Jameson's lips tenderly brushed against Candace's neck.

"Thank you," Candace whispered.

"For?"

"This. I missed you, Jameson."

"I'm right here."

"I know."

"Regrets?" Jameson asked.

"No, not regrets."

"But?"

"Realities," Candace said. Her fingertips played gently over Jameson's forearm.

"Want to talk about it?"

"There are so many potential issues," Candace said. "And, some of them have no easy solutions."

Jameson pulled Candace a little closer.

"I knew that. I understood that when I decided to do this. It's just... Now? Now, it's on my plate. It's in my hands. People don't always understand that what we do—what happens behind the facades that people see; it matters, Jameson."

"I know it does."

"Sometimes, I wonder what drives people. I think I know, and then I'm presented with some insane plot to cause injury to innocent people... I want to understand. I know that without seeking understanding, I can't make the difference I need to make."

"But?"

"But sometimes there is no time to look for common ground or to search for reasons."

Jameson let her head fall against Candace's. "I wish I could tell you that I can imagine how you feel. I can't. I can tell when you are battling with yourself. I can feel when you are struggling. You always find a way to pull people together, Candace. You do it with this family every day."

"I don't know about that."

"What happened today?"

"Nothing new," Candace replied. She moved to face Jameson. "I need this."

Jameson smiled.

"It's what keeps me steady. I need you to remind me of that."

Jameson bit her lower lip.

"Even if I bite your head off for doing that," Candace said.

"Noted," Jameson replied. "I can handle your worst."

"I'm not sure if I should take that as an insult or thank you."

"Your worst is better than anyone else's best," Jameson said.

Candace's eyes twinkled. "Are we talking about my temper?"

"Among other things."

Candace laughed. "You really are a lunatic."

"Open your fortune cookie," Jameson said.

"Why? Hoping I'll get something you can add 'in bed' to and make kinky?"

"I wouldn't complain about getting lucky."

"You don't need a fortune cookie to get lucky," Candace quipped.

Jameson took the wine glass from Candace's hand and set it aside. She placed a tender kiss on Candace's lips and handed her a fortune cookie. "Open it."

Candace raised a brow but did as Jameson directed. She cracked open the cookie and pulled out the small white paper slowly. *A new voyage will fill your life with untold memories.* Candace looked at Jameson and smiled.

"What does it say?"

"Something tells me you know the answer to that question?"

JA ARMSTRONG

"Maybe I do," Jameson confessed. "You've said the word 'sometimes' a lot tonight. Maybe sometimes you need to be reminded that you are the best person for this job."

Candace closed her eyes as Jameson's lips found hers again. Jameson understood her, not only the emotions and insecurities that she struggled with at times, but also when she needed to find the confidence to carry on. Most people looked at Candace and saw a stateswoman—a successful, powerful, controlled woman. Jameson witnessed the truth. The truth was raw and vulnerable—real—human. Confidence was not the opposite of doubt; it was the ability to press on despite questions. Confidence was born of perseverance. No one lived without insecurity. No one existed without fear. Leading required the determination to act in the face of those human frailties. Every person needed a place to voice fear, sadness, and the endless questions that seemed to have no answers—even a president. Candace had yet to assume that role. Day by day she gained a better understanding of what her life would entail. She needed Jameson to be her refuge. That had always been clear to her. She'd received a stark reminder earlier in the day. She needed the president-elect to fade away into the wife and mother that Jameson loved.

Jameson's hands tenderly caressed Candace's arms as their kiss deepened. Had she felt lonely? No. She hadn't. She was certain that Candace had.

Candace was surrounded by people twenty-four hours a day. She could scarcely enter a public bathroom without someone accompanying her. Candace seemed to take it all in stride. Jameson could see the evidence of strain on her wife's face. Candace was suddenly immersed in the details of the issues she would need to address and be accountable for the moment she took her oath of office. Solace was found in simple moments — in fortune cookies, fireplaces, children's stories, and grandchildren's antics. And, it was found in each other.

"Jameson," Candace sighed.

Jameson lowered Candace to the floor, hovering above her, searching her eyes, and smiling lovingly. It amazed Jameson; the way a simple moment of silence could transform a person. Making love with Candace would not suddenly bequeath either of them with any all-encompassing answer to life's questions. It would provide perspective. It would serve as a reminder that when the noise of contentious opinions and countless requests quelled, there remained one over-arching truth — Jameson would always love Candace, and Candace would always seek Jameson for comfort.

"I love you," Jameson promised.

Candace held Jameson's gaze as Jameson's hands deftly relieved her of her blouse. She watched as Jameson's eyes lowered and heard Jameson's sharp intake of breath. Her fingertips threaded through the soft wave of Jameson's hair, loving every moment of Jame-

son close to her. Nothing on earth moved Candace the
way it did to watch Jameson looking at her. She had
once thought that time might diminish the emotion she
witnessed in Jameson's eyes. There was no force on
earth that would ever succeed in doing that. Candace
felt that reality course through her again, astounding
her with its veracity. Her eyes closed against the sensation of Jameson's lips caressing the swell of her breasts.
Jameson's touch felt like a gentle breeze caressing the
treetops in springtime. So, gentle.

Jameson fingertips traced the path her lips had just
traversed. She pulled Candace to sit and cast aside the
bra that separated her from the treasure below. She
ached to touch Candace, to feel the softness of Candace's skin against her lips. She looked up and met
Candace's smiling face. Not for the first time, she wondered if anyone had ever loved a person as deeply as
she loved Candace. Candace's presence consumed her.
Thought was swept away by emotion. Reason? Candace was the reason — the reason Jameson looked forward to every day of her life. She loved everything
about the woman smiling at her, from the crinkles at
the corner of her eyes to the boisterous laughter that
erupted from Candace without warning. She treasured
Candace's intellect and marveled at her wife's compassion. It was strange to realize that most of the world
saw Candace Reid as a distant figure, a character that
somehow lacked dimension. Everything about Candace was real. She possessed endless layers. Jameson's

lips met Candace's tentatively, gradually beginning to explore and deepen their connection. How had she managed to become the person Candace chose to share her life with? She'd pondered that question a few times. Tonight, it seemed to surface with a new intensity.

Candace gentled their kiss and held Jameson's face in her hands. "What is it?"

Jameson wet her lips and shook her head, unable to find any words.

"Jameson..."

"I love you so much, Candace. I know that I say it. I know that you've heard it. I'm not sure you will ever understand."

Candace caressed Jameson's cheek with her thumb. "I do," she promised. "I feel the same way." She pulled Jameson's shirt over her head and tossed it away. Her eyes never left Jameson's as she continued to undress her. "Stay with me," she requested.

Jameson understood. She lowered them both to the floor again. Jameson's fingertip traced patterns cast by the flickering of the flames across Candace's skin. Her lips followed closely behind, falling like cool raindrops against the heat from the fire. She heard Candace sigh and let her mouth descend over a taut nipple. The instant arch of Candace's hips spoke directly to Jameson's heart. Sometimes, touch was the only way to convey what coursed between them. Words had their time and their purpose. Often, only the sensation of

Candace against her could satisfy the yearning that burned deep within her soul. She enveloped Candace in her arms. The heat from the crackling fire and the softness of Candace against her aroused Jameson. Her lips tasted Candace's neck and meandered lower as they began to glide sensually against each other. Candace's perfume tickled her nose. She breathed in the scent, savoring the way it caused her heart to beat slightly out of time. Candace's hands fell over her back tenderly, moving in long strokes, pulling Jameson closer.

Dear God. Candace held onto Jameson. Jameson's lips surrounded her nipple, a playful graze of Jameson's teeth took her breath away. A fingertip danced over her collarbone as Jameson's mouth continued its thorough exploration of her breasts. Candace fell away into a well of sensation; a well that overflowed and spilled out everywhere around them, between them, even through them. She would drown here and never regret it. Jameson would always pull her back to the surface. After all, wasn't that the most glorious part of making love? Lost one moment, desperate and searching; found in the next, cradled and comforted; making love with Jameson was always that way.

Jameson's hand found the softness between Candace's legs. Soft, warm, wet from desire—it spurred Jameson's need. She glanced up to a sight unlike any other. *Candace.*

Candace's head had fallen back exposing her throat. Her eyes were shut tightly; her lips parted in anticipation. Barely audible sighs mixed with sensual moans, carrying to Jameson's ears like chords in a beautiful melody. There was no sight on earth that compared to Candace in the throes of passion. Sunsets, sunrises, mountains, and oceans be damned; the most breathtaking vision in creation was laid before Jameson now.

Tenderly, Jameson entered Candace. A guttural moan rewarded her. Jameson entered Candace gently at first; deeper and harder with each thrust until Candace's hips rotated to meet her endeavor. A flurry of kisses rained over Candace's stomach to her hip, until finally Jameson's tongue languidly traveled over her center, lingering when it met with the fingers still twirling inside her. Candace might not survive this night after all. Quivers erupted in her core, spreading like sparks through every nerve in her body. Tingles ran over her skin. Was it the heat of the fire or the heat from Jameson's tongue? Maybe it was the feel of Jameson's breasts against her thigh, or perhaps, it was the fullness of Jameson's fingers as they continued to press deeper that was responsible. It was all of it, every tiny sensation meeting the other like instruments in a symphony. One played a beautiful note; together they created a haunting refrain that echoed through Candace's being. Her hands gripped Jameson's shoulders as the crescendo that heralds the end of a melody built steadily within her.

Jameson relished the sights, the sounds, and the taste that was uniquely Candace. She continued her tender assault, in and out, up and down; her other hand reached for Candace's breast. She delighted in the tremors that began the moment her fingertip brushed across Candace's nipple. She ceased her teasing and sucked delicately on Candace's clit until the tremors broke like waves, crashing violently over and over, one behind the other.

Candace's body lifted from the floor. She was certain the only thing that kept her from levitating was the weight of Jameson's body on hers. She called out Jameson's name repeatedly. Jameson would not relent. "Oh, God… Jameson… Jesus Christ!"

Jameson licked and played and teased until Candace shuddered beneath her again. She could do this forever.

Candace couldn't stand another moment. She wanted Jameson above her. She wanted to taste Jameson, to make her quiver and shake until she had no choice but to fall into Candace's waiting arms. She tugged on Jameson's shoulders. Jameson's lips met hers. Candace groaned. Everything about Jameson was sexy. Jameson's tongue explored her mouth just as it had peeked her arousal seconds ago. She pushed Jameson away slightly, and licked her lips.

"Yes?" Jameson asked.

"I want to taste you right now."

Jameson thought she would orgasm right there. Lust blazed in Candace's eyes, hotter than the flames of the fire a few feet away.

Candace guided Jameson above her. She loved to place Jameson here, where she could reach her hands up and toy with Jameson's nipples while her mouth explored all that Jameson had to offer. She greeted Jameson eagerly. Tonight, she had no desire to prolong Jameson's torture. She desired to release Jameson, to feel Jameson let go of all control.

"Candace," Jameson moaned her wife's name. "Oh, that... Oh, my God... Yes..."

Jameson was gone. Candace took her over the edge. Her fingers tugged at Jameson's nipples, and her tongue swirled around Jameson's clit repeatedly, tenderly but firmly.

"Candace!"

Jameson grabbed hold of the couch with one hand to keep from losing her balance. She had no intention of pulling away. As long as Candace wanted to keep her suspended, she would oblige.

"Mmm." Candace felt her arousal building again. Every quiver from Jameson's body seemed to cause a tremor in Candace. She felt Jameson beginning to succumb again and dropped her hand to touch herself. She couldn't stand the ache any longer. She needed to crest and fall with Jameson.

Jameson's heart thundered in her ears. She could feel Candace touching herself and it sent shock waves through her. She wished she could watch Candace now, but Candace would never allow it. Desire silenced all Jameson's inhibitions. "You're touching yourself," she panted. The only response from Candace was a desperate moan. "Oh, God... I wish I could watch you," Jameson confessed.

Candace almost lost it. Jameson seldom spoke un-prompted when Candace touched her. She struggled to voice her desires. Tonight, it seemed, she was at their mercy. It made Candace crave release. She prayed Jameson's voice would continue to reach her ears.

"Yes," Jameson hissed. She swirled her hips over Candace's face. "Please," she nearly begged. "Candace... I want you to make yourself come with me... Please... God, I want you... I want to feel you.... Oh!" Jameson's words sent them both over the edge of sanity.

Candace shifted and accepted Jameson into her arms.

"Jesus," Jameson sighed.

Candace chuckled. "Finding God?"

Jameson looked at Candace. "Hey, I like this version of Bible Study."

"You're nuts."

"I love you."

"I love you too," Candace replied. She looked at Jameson curiously. "What are you thinking?"

"I hope all the fireplaces work in The White House."

Candace burst out laughing. "All of them?"

Jameson nodded.

"A little ambitious?"

"Nah. There's twenty-eight. We'll be there for forty-eight months. That's like what? About 1.7 fireplaces a month. Doable."

Candace stared at Jameson for a moment before laughing again. "Lunatic."

"Hey, you're not the only one with plans."

"Thank God." Candace pulled Jameson close and let her eyes close.

"Do you want to go upstairs?" Jameson asked.

"Not yet."

"Okay…. So, which one do you want to try out first?" Jameson asked.

Candace shook with laughter. "You're the architect, honey. Draw up a plan."

Jameson grinned and snuggled against Candace. "I will."

I have no doubt.

CHAPTER TWO

"Are you sure about this?" Grant asked.

Candace was growing tired of that simple question.

"I'm just asking," he said, sensing her displeasure.

"Nate and I have discussed this at length," she said. "We both agree that Senator Gorham is the best choice for Secretary of State."

Grant nodded.

"Unless there is something I don't know that I should know, that is my decision."

"No, there's not. Jenny is a logical choice."

"Jenny Gorham is more than a logical choice, Grant. She's one of the most well-versed people on foreign policy in leadership today. And, she happens to speak four languages fluently. That's an enormous bonus on the world stage."

"And, she's a woman."

"Your point?"

"Did that tip the scales in her favor? I think some people will ask that."

"Some people will ask a lot of things."

Grant groaned. "Candy…"

Candace held up her hand. "Don't. Gender is neither a qualifying or disqualifying factor in this administration. You, of all people, should know that."

"This isn't about what *I* know."

"Then what is it about?"

"Whether you like it or not, perception still matters."

Candace took a deep breath and exhaled slowly. She understood with crystal clarity how important optics were on the world stage. Like it or not, optics mattered. Optics were also a fickle thing. People perceived any situation differently based on their firmly held convictions and embedded beliefs. No candidate, no leader, and no president would ever be able to create perfect "optics." She'd attempted to school her staff in that reality. At times, it seemed that remedial lessons were called for. That frustrated Candace. She listened thoughtfully to the guidance of her advisers, both at work and at home. She listened. When she made a decision, it was solid. Spending time explaining her reasoning or debating her choices was not a luxury she was afforded. Each day, Candace received nearly the same security briefing President Wallace did. Every morning, she listened to and accepted calls from congressional and foreign leaders seeking her support and offering theirs. And, in the afternoon she engaged in meetings to formalize her inauguration. She was grateful that Jameson had taken control of their move to Washington DC. While she still needed to address details regarding their living quarters, Jameson had handled nearly everything. That took a few hours off each day. Each day seemed to be composed of forty-eight hours of tasks poured into twenty-four hours of time. She did not appreciate revisiting decisions that required no further discussion.

"Grant," she began evenly. "I think we need to establish something."

"What's that?"

"I love you, and I am grateful for your insight and your candor."

"But?"

"I told you; as I told everyone during the campaign; when I make a decision, unless there is some earth-shattering information that makes that decision perilous, I don't have the time to revisit it." She held up her hand to stop his oncoming thought. "Ultimately, the success or the failure of any decision in my administration will rest with me, just as it did during the campaign. I expect that everyone on my team is honest with me. And, I welcome spirited debate — when we are in that phase of the decision-making process. That process has an end. It's called the decision. I take everything that's offered to me into consideration. Once I have made that decision, I expect respect for the conclusion I have reached. The government has enough built-in redundancies. We can't afford to create more."

"I'm only trying to look out for you."

Candace smiled. Grant was like a son to her. His eyes had lowered, reminding her of a child who had been reprimanded. Sometimes, governing mirrored parenting a great deal. She would forever be amazed at how adults could transform into small children. She often felt the same way in Pearl's presence. "I realize that. You need to trust that when I've arrived at my decision, it's been through plenty of internal debate. Jenny isn't just a logical choice. She's the right choice for this administration. Optics matter, Grant. They fade into nothingness if they lack any substance behind them."

"Understood."

"Good. Now, where are we at with face-time for Health and Human Services candidates?"

"John Beringer is Saturday at two. Derek Benton at four..."

"Push it to five."

"Candy..."

"Push it to five, Grant. I want time with Beringer."

"Are you seriously considering him?"

For the second time in a few minutes, Candace thought her head might explode. *That doesn't deserve a response.* "Push it to five." *God, give me strength.*

⚜

"Where's Mom?" Michelle asked when she entered the kitchen.

"Hello, to you too, Shell," Jameson said.

"Yeah, yeah. Seriously. Where's Mom?"

"She's in the study with Grant."

"Today? It's Thanksgiving."

"Yes, I know. She was up at four getting the turkey ready."

"What time did Grant get here?"

"Seven."

"Has she been with him all that time?" Michelle asked.

Jameson didn't comment; indicating her displeasure with the situation.

"It's almost eleven."

"Yeah, well, they have a lot to deal with."

Michelle groaned. "She could have one day off."

"I don't think so," Jameson said. "That's not the way it works, Shell. We all knew that."

"Yeah, but it's Thanksgiving."

"And, she has a few weeks to assemble her team. She's got people coming here Saturday."

Shell shook her head. "I thought we were all coming over Saturday?"

"You are."

"I'm missing something."

"Well, you'll be missing her in the afternoon. From what she told me, she's got face-to-face talks with HHS candidates."

"At least, she's narrowing things down, JD."

"Mmm."

"You okay?"

"Me? Sure," Jameson said.

"I'm serious," Michelle said.

"So am I. I'm fine, Shell. I just worry about the pace she's keeping sometimes."

"Mom will be okay."

"Talking about me?" Candace walked up and pecked Jameson on the cheek. "Did you check on my turkey?"

"Yes, I checked on the turkey." Jameson chuckled. "Maybe you should go rest before everyone gets here."

"I'm okay." Candace laughed at the doubtful gazes of her wife and daughter. "Good Lord, you two; I've had longer, more stressful days." She looked at Michelle. "I did give birth to you."

"Funny, Mom."

"I thought so," Candace said.

"Momma!" Cooper scurried into the room and headed straight for Jameson.

Candace smiled. Jameson's eyes always lit up like a Christmas tree when Cooper called for her. *No more work today.*

"What's up, Coop?" Jameson asked.

"Me and Spence need your help."

"My help?"

"Yeah." He pulled Jameson down to whisper in her ear.

Jameson's hand covered her mouth to keep from laughing.

Candace's brow immediately arched. *Now, what is that about, I wonder?*

"Okay, Coop," Jameson said. "I'll be right there."

"'Kay!" Cooper started to run away and stopped. "Hi, Mommy."

"Hi, Cooper."

"Hey, what am I? Chopped liver or something?" Shell asked.

Cooper giggled. "Hi, Shell."

"Yeah, yeah," Michelle grumbled.

Cooper giggled some more and ran off.

"Care to tell us what you are being summoned for?" Candace asked.

"Nope, but I think Shell should get the camera on her phone ready and sneak in behind me."

"Why am I suddenly afraid to ask?" Candace said.

"I'm not!" Michelle grabbed her phone from her pocket. "We'll be right behind you," she told Jameson.

Candace rolled her eyes. "You two are a bad influence on each other."

"You're just figuring that out now?" Michelle asked. She grabbed Candace's hand. "Come on, I know you're as curious as I am."

After a beat, Candace allowed Michelle to lead her away. *Oh, no.* Candace could not suppress her laughter. Grant was tangled in a mess of — what was Grant tangled in? Yarn? Where on earth did Cooper and Spencer find yarn?

"Oh, laugh it up!" Grant groaned.

"Why is Grant tied up on the floor?" Michelle asked.

"Because," Cooper said. "He 'napped Mommy."

"He what?" Michelle asked.

"He kidnapped Mommy," Jameson explained.

Candace shook with laughter. Visions of Nate Ellison or some foreign dignitary tied to a chair in the West Wing flooded her brain. *God, help them all.*

"Why are you laughing?" Grant asked. "I'm tied up! In *pink* yarn!"

"I don't know, I think pink is good on you," Jameson offered.

"JD!" He pleaded.

"Ohhhh my," Melanie opened the front door and lifted the twins' stroller inside. "What happened to you?"

"They did." Grant tried to point while he untangled himself from a sea of fluorescent pink squiggles. "I thought you were helping?" He looked at Jameson.

Jameson shrugged. "They didn't ask me to help free you," she explained.

Grant shed the last vestiges of his pink cocoon. "I'm glad you're all so amused."

"Hey, don't kidnap Mom and you'll be fine," Michelle offered.

Candace laughed some more. "I'm going to get moving on the rest of dinner."

"I'll help," Michelle offered.

Jameson shook her head. "How did you manage to let them capture you?"

Grant groaned. "They told me they wanted me to help with a fort, and then they turned on me."

Jameson laughed. "Did you learn anything?"

"Yeah, I'm not having any kids — ever."

"Never say never, Grant. Trust me on that; never say never."

Pearl cornered Candace at the sink. "How are you holding up?"

"I'm tired," Candace admitted. There was no point in denying anything to Pearl. If anyone could see through Candace's façade it was the woman next to her.

"Feel like a little walk?"

Candace nodded. "I have to…"

"I know. No more escaping unnoticed."

"No."

"How about we hide in the pantry and have a glass of wine?" Pearl suggested playfully.

"Don't tempt me."

"I guess it's the kitchen table," Pearl said. "The kids all seem to be otherwise engaged."

"I'll pour the wine," Candace said.

"So?" Pearl urged gently. "Want to talk about whatever it is you don't want any of those fools in the other room to know?"

"I wouldn't know where to begin," Candace replied honestly. "I will miss this."

Pearl nodded. "You'll still have this, Candy. You will just be in a different big white house."

"True."

"But I think I understand what you mean. I think we'll all miss it a little. You might be surprised how much you will enjoy the new surroundings."

Candace tipped her head. "Maybe."

"You were meant for this, Candy," Pearl said.

Candace was stunned by the comment. Pearl had always encouraged her to stretch and to make her dreams into goals. She'd been Candace's biggest cheerleader and her most trusted confidante for a lifetime. The presidency hadn't been Candace's lifelong aspiration. When it became a viable possibility, Candace found herself compelled to make it a reality. There were countless reasons she sought the job she was about to assume. Much of it was because she believed she could handle it, and she wanted a chance to make a difference. Part of her was enticed by the historic nature of her candidacy and what would be her presidency. She'd be lying if she claimed that the notion of being the first woman to hold the highest office in the land hadn't been alluring. She had never considered herself a vain person, but Candace had always been ambitious. Ambition was a necessary trait for anyone who wanted to seek the presidency. It was not the only attribute a person needed to possess; resilience was equally important.

"You look surprised," Pearl said.

"I am. I never seriously considered this until a few years ago."

"I'm aware."

"Then what makes you think I was meant for this?"

"You were. What do you want me to do; give you a laundry list of the reasons why?"

Candace shrugged.

"All you ever wanted was to be in politics, Candy. You used to practice making speeches in the yard."

Candace chuckled.

"You were reading legislation in junior high school when most girls your age were reading Judy Blume."

"That sounds truly terrible," Candace admitted. "No wonder I didn't have many dates."

Pearl laughed. "I think you came out on top in that department."

Candace winked. Pearl adored Jameson, and Pearl was right. It had taken Candace longer than many people to find love that would last. She'd found that with Jameson. She'd never been a believer in soulmates. For Candace, that concept over-simplified the complexities of love and relationships. Love existed on its own. It was born without your permission. In order for love to blossom and grow in a relationship it has to be nurtured. Love was the flower in a garden full of roots and weeds. It could become choked without care. Jameson understood that. They worked at their marriage. When the weeds started to take hold, they took the time to pull them up and repair the hole left behind. No marriage was perfect. Candace had found what most eluded most people for a lifetime. She'd fallen in love with someone who was equally committed to tending the garden, even when it got messy. "Yes, I did."

"I can't tell you that I can imagine what you are feeling."

"I'm not having any regrets," Candace said. "Facing it; looking at what I've agreed to take on, it's — well, it's daunting, Mom."

"I'll bet. Scared?"

"Terrified." Candace chuckled. "But, also excited."

Pearl's lips crinkled with amusement. She was excited for Candace, and proud of her daughter. Candace was her daughter. "I understand that. It's a bit terrifying to watch your daughter become the president."

Candace smiled.

"I can't tell you how proud I am of you."

"Mom…"

"No, it's the truth. And, not just because you won an election. You are the right person, Candy."

"Well, I may need you to remind me of that from time to time."

"Happy to. How are things moving along?"

"You mean with the transition?"

"And everything else."

"As smoothly as it can, I think. Thank God for Jameson. If I had to deal with thinking about furniture, I think I might find myself in a big house with barbed wire instead of iron gates."

Pearl laughed. "Grant is driving you nuts."

"He means well."

"Mmm."

"What?"

"He wants to protect you."

"Yes, I know."

"How are things between him and Jessica?"

Candace sighed. She still cared deeply for her former partner, and she loved Grant. Jessica wrestled with profound guilt over her decision to place Grant for adoption. He'd ended up with a family who had provided well for him. It was not a family in which he felt validated. His adoptive parents' religious beliefs bordered on obsessive in Candace's view. Grant's decision to pursue a relationship with Jessica, and worse, with Candace, had severely damaged his relationship with the people who had raised him. He carried fear

and insecurity about both her and Jessica, and he har-
bored resentment for his parents.

"It's not easy," Candace said. "For either of
them. Jessica loves him so much. She does. He loves
her. There's so much emotional baggage for them both.
He's afraid of losing her. She blames herself for that
fear."

"And you?"

"Me? You know that I think of Grant as a son as
much as I did Rick or Scott, or any of my kids for that
matter."

"Yes, I do. And, Jessica?"

"I wish she'd give herself a chance."

"You're going to keep him on your staff; aren't
you?"

Candace nodded. "It's not only the personal
part. Grant is one of the smartest people I know. He has
a knack for knowing how people will react. He's a lot
like…"

"His mother?"

"Yeah. Why so many questions about Grant?"

"No reason."

"Right. You always have a reason."

"Do you trust him, Candy?"

"I do."

"Okay."

"You don't? Even after all this time?"

"I didn't say that," Pearl replied. "All the baggage—Candy, that all carries weight. I just don't want you to get injured when he starts to unload it."

Candace sighed. Jameson had raised similar concerns. She could pretend that they had no merit; she wouldn't. Anything that Pearl or Jameson expressed as a concern warranted her attention. "I know."

"Good." Pearl changed the subject. "So, what do you think?"

"About?"

"Think there will be a wedding in that new white house your moving into?"

Candace grinned. Marianne and Scott seemed to be heading toward making a commitment. She was not only relieved that Marianne had found someone again, she was thrilled that it was Scott. Scott loved Marianne. He also accepted her children as his. His presence in Jameson's life meant the world to Jameson. Candace loved happy endings. Not every ending was happy. Both Scott and Marianne had received painful lessons in that reality. Simply put, they fit. "I hope so," she said.

"Tired?" Jameson asked when she crawled into bed.

"Exhausted."

"It was a good day."

"It was," Candace agreed.

"I can't wait to send Grant those photos Shell took."

"You have an evil streak."

"Nah. I just like to bust his balls."

"I noticed." Candace grew serious.

"Something wrong?" Jameson wondered.

"I don't know. Pearl said something today."

"Pearl said a lot of things today."

Candace laughed. Pearl had consumed a few glasses of wine; enough that she was sleeping in Jonah's old room.

"Something tells me I was not a party to what you're talking about," Jameson surmised.

"Grant."

"What about him?" Jameson asked.

"You were worried when he came into the picture."

"I was."

"Are you now?" Candace asked.

"Candace, is there something going on that you haven't told me?"

"No."

Jameson nodded. "Am I worried about Grant working for you?"

"Yes."

"I'm not worried that he'll betray you, if that's what you mean."

Candace remained silent.

"Are you?" Jameson wanted to know. "Are you worried that he'll turn back to his roots?"

"No. You are concerned about him, though," Candace guessed.

"I keep my eyes open where you're concerned."

"I know that."

"I know what he means to you, and I know that things between him and Jess have been a little…"

"Strained?"

"Yeah. I also know that Jess is someone you care about."

"She is."

"She's been a good friend to both of us, Candace. I don't want your relationship with him to hurt what you and Jess have managed to cultivate. There's a lot of history with you two."

"All true," Candace admitted. "I can't explain it. I feel like he needs this."

"And, you feel responsible."

"I wouldn't say that."

"No, you wouldn't, but you do. You've felt responsible for him for years. You have some crazy idea that if it weren't for you he'd have been able to make things work with his parents."

Candace sighed. That was the truth.

"Look, you have enough responsibility, Candace. I know you love Grant. I get it. I think we all love Grant now."

Candace smiled.

"We all love Jess too. But you have the entire world looking to you, not to mention four kids, a slew of grandchildren, and me. You can't take on all of Grant and Jessica's shit. You can try and help and guide; you can't fix everything. It isn't just Jessica carrying guilt."

"So, you don't have an issue with Grant being on my staff?"

"No," Jameson said. "Your administration is your call, Candace. If you ask me, I will give you an honest opinion. You and I both know that will be based more on impression than on any political savvy."

"I think you sell yourself short there."

"Nope. I don't. That's your expertise. When you want to make a decision that's about our family, that's a different ballgame. Don't second-guess yourself on that decision, not even based on Pearl."

Candace leaned in and kissed Jameson lovingly. "Thank you."

"Anytime." Jameson laid back and pulled Candace into her arms.

"Speaking of ball games," Candace said.

"Yeah?"

"I think they're going to ask me to throw out the first pitch at the National's opener next season." Jameson snickered.

"Why are you laughing?"

"I'm not."

"Jameson!"

"When was the last time you threw a baseball?"

"I don't know."

Jameson cleared her throat.

"What?"

"You might want to find a catcher for practice."

"You don't think I can get the ball across the plate, do you?"

Jameson said nothing.

Candace sat up. "You don't. I don't believe it. I got elected President of the United States, and you don't think I'm capable of pitching a baseball across home plate!"

"I'm just saying that you might want to practice."

Candace huffed. "I thought you trusted my judgment."

"I do. It's your pitching arm I'm worried about."

Candace frowned.

Jameson held up her hands in surrender.

Surrendering already? Candace climbed on top of Jameson. "We'll just see how many bases you can cover."

Jameson's eyes flashed with excitement, and she flipped Candace beneath her. "Starting at first?" She kissed Candace. "I think I might just slide into home," she whispered.

Candace giggled and pulled Jameson down for another kiss. *I love baseball.*

CHAPTER THREE

"JD?"

Jameson lifted her head to the sound of Dana's voice. "Hey."

"Sorry, if I'm interrupting."

"Nothing more than looking for furniture for Cooper."

"Still dealing with the move?"

"You know, I don't know why, but my whole life I just assumed people moved into the White House and it was all furnished for them."

Dana laughed. "You could've moved the furniture you have."

"We are. Some of it. Everything we're bringing from New York will arrive here next week."

"Where are you going to put it?"

Jameson laughed. She'd yet to figure that all out yet. The cost of moving into the White House fell to the first family. Marianne was still living in the house in Schoharie. There was no way that Candace would want to take much from their home there. The few things they had purchased for the Governor's Mansion in

New York had either been moved into the farmhouse or they had been donated to charity. The townhouse seemed the logical place to move from. Jameson had always loved Candace's townhouse in Virginia. They would be taking a substantial number of items from their current residence—not the children's furniture. Candace and Jameson intended to offer the townhouse to Jonah and Laura. They'd yet to broach the idea.

"I have no idea where it's going to go," Jameson confessed. "I guess that depends on Jonah and Laura."

"Why?"

"Candace and I are going to offer them this place."

"Seriously?"

"Yeah. I was looking to open an office down here before I left the firm. Mel and Jonah have been considering that option for a while. All these babies have slowed things down."

"That, and their mother running for the presidency."

"And, that."

"If there's anything I can do..."

"Don't you have enough on your plate?"

"Probably." Dana laughed.

"How is my wife these days?"

"Haven't seen her much, huh?"

"Not really. Late nights, early mornings."

"I'd get used to that."

"I am. I'm just glad she's been sleeping."

Candace had been rolling into bed in the wee hours for over a week. If she wasn't in a briefing, she was on a call with a potential cabinet member. If it wasn't dealing with the cabinet, she was in a meeting about the inauguration. And, if it wasn't that, she was making calls to congressional allies. She'd made a point to pull herself away every day for a couple of hours to spend with Cooper, usually over dinner. Jameson had no idea how Candace kept up with everything. In a few weeks, there would be no move to coordinate, and no inauguration demanding Candace's attention. The cabinet appointments would be solidified. That was the silver lining Jameson could see. When Candace did roll into bed, exhaustion claimed her immediately. Jameson was grateful for that. It meant that Candace felt confident in the decisions she was making on a daily basis.

"Missing her, huh?" Dana guessed.

"I miss her when she's gone for a few hours, Dana."

"You've still got it bad, JD."

Jameson winked. *Yep.* "You didn't come find me to discuss Coop's bedroom or my infatuation with my wife. What's up?"

"As interesting as both those things are, no, I didn't."

"I'm listening," Jameson said.

"Candy wants you to pick the song for the Inaugural Balls."

"The song?"

"Yeah, the one you dance to with her."

Jameson stared at Dana blankly.

"Hello? Earth to JD."

"Why didn't she ask me?"

Dana offered Jameson a compassionate smile. "She said you'd ask that."

"And?"

"She said she tried to this morning."

"She did?"

"Yeah."

"Really?"

"You told her you were awake."

"Uh oh." Jameson could be a heavy sleeper. She also talked in her sleep. "What did I say?"

"Ummm…"

"Dana?"

"I believe the word jiggy was in the title."

Jameson cringed. "Not really appropriate, huh?"

"Hey, you two are breaking every tradition I know. I say, let's get jiggy with it."

Jameson laughed.

"Anyway, she wanted to ask you. Brandon and Donna were riding her about it earlier. Details, you know? Apparently, that's an important one to them."

"It's over a month away," Jameson said.

"Yeah, well, there's the holidays in between. Ten Inaugural Balls, JD. There's a schedule and there's only so much time. We need to know so we can coordinate with…"

"I get it. When do they need to know?"

"By the 20th, if you can."

"Sure. Hey, Dana?"

"Yeah?"

"Does she have to know?"

"What?"

"Candace, does she have to know what I choose?"

"You want to keep the song a secret from the president?"

Jameson wiggled her eyebrows. "Can we?"

"Are you trying to get me fired?"

"Oh, come on!"

"Tell me this first."

"Okay…"

"You're not going to choose to get jiggy for real, are you?"

"Not at the balls."

Dana rolled her eyes. "I'll see what I can do."

Jameson grinned.

"I said, I'll see what I can do."

"You'll figure it out." Jameson turned back to her computer screen.

"Yeah. And, JD?"

Jameson looked up.

"No sexual healing either."

Jameson shrugged. "Sounds like you need to spend some more time with Steve."

Dana threw a pillow from a chair at her friend.

"Violence won't solve anything. Haven't you listened to any of your boss' speeches?"

"You're a pain in my ass," Dana said.

"Love you too," Jameson called after her.

"I mean it, JD! No bump and grind either!" Dana exchanged a grin with Candace in the hallway.

Jameson sniggered as she returned to her task. "Oh, there'll be plenty of grinding."

"Planning a new project?"

Jameson looked up and froze.

"Now, I know I don't want to know. Tell me anyway," Candace said.

"How come you didn't tell me you wanted me to pick the song for us to dance to?"

"I tried."

"Yeah, I heard. You could've tried again."

"Are you upset?"

"No."

"Jameson?"

"No, I just wish you would've asked me yourself."

"If you want to know the truth, I think Dana wanted a chance to tease you."

"Shocking," Jameson replied.

"She and Steve miss you, Jameson."

"I see Dana all the time."

"I know you do. Maybe you should make some time to spend with Steve."

Jameson sat back in her chair. Steve Russo was her best friend from college and Dana's husband. They remained close friends, but they had spent less and less time together over the last few years. It wasn't intentional. It was life. They saw each other at functions and family parties. Jameson had to admit she couldn't easily recall the last time she'd called Steve just to catch up. If it hadn't been for Steve and Dana, she'd likely never have known Candace.

"Is everything okay with Dana and Steve?"

"I think so," Candace said. She flopped into a chair. "Another move. It takes its toll. You know that as well as anyone."

Jameson decided against delving into the topic. Moving was stressful; moving with a child added to that tension. Steve and Dana had two kids to consider, and to make feel secure. "Not that I'm not happy to see you…"

"But what am I doing out of my cell?" Candace asked. She received a slight shrug from Jameson. "President Wallace invited us to lunch on Monday."

"Okay."

Candace smiled. Jameson could roll with the punches better than anyone she knew.

"On one condition," Jameson said.

Candace waited.

"I get to keep the song a secret."

Candace was stunned. "You're not serious?"

"I'm completely serious."

"You want me to walk out on stage without knowing what we're dancing to?"

"Worried?"

"A little," Candace confessed.

"I thought you liked to bump and grind."

"Jameson!" Candace laughed. "Why don't you want me to know?"

Jameson sighed. There were moments when Jameson felt helpless. They were only moments. Candace cast a long shadow. She dealt with things that Jameson could scarcely comprehend, much less hope to control. A song choice might seem insignificant to most people. Jameson saw the opportunity as a way to give something to Candace on a day that would be one of the most significant in all their lives. It was something she could contribute. "Maybe I would like to be able to do something for you that day."

"Jameson, you do more for me than anyone in this world every day. Surprise me," she said.

Jameson smiled. "Thanks."

"I only have one request."

"What's that?"

"Choose something I can maneuver in heels."

Jameson laughed. Candace could walk a tightrope in heels if she had to. Jameson, on the other hand, searched for any and all alternatives to heels. "I'll keep your request in mind."

"You do that." Candace forced herself to leave the comfort of the chair.

"Back at it?" Jameson guessed.

"For a little while."

"Mm-hum."

"I'll see you at dinner." *I can't imagine what she's going to choose.*

🎗🎗

MONDAY

Jameson couldn't keep her eyes from sweeping over the majesty of the White House. She'd visited numerous times with Candace. Today felt different. This would be her home in a little over a month. Not for the first time, she found herself amazed by her life —amazed by the woman who shared her life. How many presidents had there been? Forty-four? Forty-four in more than two centuries. Jameson shook her head to clear the thought.

"Are you okay?" Candace asked softly.

Jameson's only reply was a wink and smile. *I can't believe it.* Today it all felt real. She'd watched advisers come and go over the last month. She had shaken hands with nearly every leader in the Democratic party over the last two years. Candace was about to become *their* leader. "Crazy," she muttered.

Candace looked at Jameson and snickered. "Just hitting you?"

Jameson smiled again. "Something like that. You?"

Candace took a breath as the car rolled to a stop. Had it hit her yet? She wasn't certain how to answer that question. Her days had already changed markedly. She was privy to information that only a handful of people on the planet were granted access to review. She was engaged in building a branch of the most powerful government in the world. Candace wondered if the reality would ever fully be realized for her. She felt the gravity of it all. For Candace, focusing on what needed to be done, who needed to be courted and who needed to be kept in line dictated her current thoughts. The job of a president entailed more than making speeches or signing pieces of legislation. Shortly, she would become Commander in Chief; the leader of a military comprised of men and women volunteering to serve their country. She would be responsible for people willingly sacrificing the freedoms they sought to defend for others, and potentially paying an unthinkable price for that service. She thought about that every morning when she woke. People would trust her to act with conscience and clarity.

The President of the United States also served as the country's chief diplomat. Every word that Candace spoke in the world stage would have the power to inspire, alienate, or attract the people of other nations and that nation's leaders. That required at the very least a cursory understanding of each country's government, geography, and geology. All of that impacted economy and culture. If Candace hoped to cultivate a healthy relationship with allies and draw adversaries closer, she would need to be deliberate and thoughtful with rhetoric. Words held power. Candace would also serve as Chief Legislator, Chief Executive, Chief of the Democratic Party, and perhaps most important of all, she would become Chief Citizen. It was her responsibility to represent and lead an entire nation, not merely those who gathered in her corner. Regardless of how anyone cast their vote, if they cast a vote at all, where they lived in the country, how they worshiped, looked, where they worked, their age or their gender, Candace was charged with acting in their best interest and representing their needs in the discharge of her duties. It was a daunting task. It was a task she welcomed.

"I don't know," she told Jameson. "I just know that it can never appear that I'm not in command — even now."

Jameson watched as the door opened and Candace stepped out. President Wallace and his wife, Marion, were standing outside waiting to greet them. She heard the clicks of cameras in the distance and smiled at the official White House photographer as she accepted Candace's hand and stepped out of the car. *Here we go.*

"Candy." President Wallace hugged Candace. "Ready for this place?"

"Let's hope so," she replied lightly.

"JD," the president greeted Jameson. He hugged her next. "I can't wait to see what this place looks like when you're done," he whispered.

"I think Cooper and Spencer might have a bigger effect," Jameson quipped.

The president laughed. "Probably so. Let's go in and escape the cameras for a few minutes."

Jameson was grateful. She'd learned to take the press in stride as much as anyone could. She preferred the quiet of home to the clicking of cameras and the shouting of questions. She stepped beside the First Lady.

"How are you holding up, JD?" Marion asked.

"I've considered crutches a few times," Jameson replied cheekily.

Marion laughed. "You don't need to tell me. What do you say to a beer?"

"I'm not driving."

Marion laughed harder. She was fond of Jameson. She'd known Candace for years. Senator Don Wallace and Senator Candace Fletcher had campaigned together for President John Merrow. They had both taken the lead in persuading President Lawrence Strickland to forego a presidential campaign. He had succeeded Merrow to the office after President Merrow's assassination. Both Don Wallace and Candace regarded Strickland as eager, imprudent, and at times, irrational. His exit from office had paved the way for eight years of a Wallace administration. It hardly surprised Marion that President Don Wallace would be followed by President Candace Reid. Both were built for leadership. Marion had witnessed evidence of her husband's and Candace's strength and dexterity countless times over the years. Being a president's spouse carried its own set of complications and contradictions. The public craved someone it perceived as genuine, the job demanded its occupant maintain composure. She'd struggled at points during her husband's time holding the nation's highest office. She had the unique vantage point to see the cracks in his control. She'd watched him shed tears in private and pound his fist on his desk. She'd felt the empty space beside her in the middle of the night more times than she cared to count. She'd boarded planes and trains, waved from cars, and shaken hands with factory workers and prime ministers across the globe. The role of First Lady was one of Supporter in Chief. It could be exhausting one minute and exhilarating the next. It was not a role for the faint of heart.

Marion stopped to bid her husband and Candace a temporary farewell. "I'm going to steal your wife while you two talk about whatever it is you two talk about," she told Candace.

Candace chuckled. "If I know you, you'll be drinking beer with my wife while we..."

"Drink scotch?" Marion quipped.

"I think I might know where there's a bottle," the president offered. "We'll see you two in an hour." He leaned in and kissed Marion on the cheek.

Candace squeezed Jameson's hand. "Don't do anything I wouldn't do," she whispered playfully.

Jameson's eyes gleamed. *There are so many things I want to say right now.* She placed a sweet kiss on Candace's cheek. "See you at lunch."

Marion shook her head when the president and his incoming successor walked away. "If only the world knew how much trouble those two could cause together." She giggled. "So, what about that beer I promised?"

"I'm game."

"I thought we could relax in the rec room we have on the third floor before we have to engage in all the formalities." She led Jameson through the house. "I'm sure you have plenty of ideas about what you'd like to use that space for."

"Not really," Jameson said.

"Really? I thought you'd be excited to make changes."

Jameson shrugged. "Candace and I have looked at the important public spaces. She's got an eye for things that she doesn't think she has."

"And, what about your space?"

Jameson sighed. "Well, I think we might keep the rec room idea. Modify it a bit for the kids."

"Kids?"

"Oh, no." Jameson laughed. "No new additions from me. But we have all the grandkids and Coop. I swear they get bigger by the minute. Cooper will be seven this year. Spencer will be six. I don't know how that happened."

"It goes by faster with each day," Marion agreed. "That's why I wanted to have a space up here for the family to unwind. Our four grandkids are growing like weeds too. Sometimes, when our kids are here, they seem to have gone in the other direction."

Jameson chuckled. She understood Marion's meaning intimately. She thought it was interesting to watch Candace's kids. They were all fantastic parents by Jameson's account. She continued to marvel at the way they became children in Candace's presence. Becoming part of Candace's family had given Jameson a new perspective on life and love. She'd seen the same transformation happen to Candace when Pearl was close. And, she now recognized that she too sought out her mother for comfort and encouragement as she did when she was a child. A person grew taller, gained experience, and learned how to navigate the world as an adult; no one ever ceased to need the love and acceptance of the person or people who had raised them. Jameson counted herself lucky. She had amazing parents. She considered herself blessed to be Candace's wife. Candace loved her children more than anything in the world, and that had allowed Jameson to venture into a world she'd never dreamed she'd have a chance to experience. Jameson cherished being Cooper's mother. She'd fallen in love with each of Candace's children, and when all was said and done, they had become hers too.

"I know what you mean," Jameson said.

"I'll tell you the truth," Marion began. She opened the door to the rec room on the third floor. "The kids are what has kept us sane these last eight years."

Jameson was curious.

"Living here, you gain a new appreciation for the chaos of family. I'm not sure how to explain it."

Jameson smiled at the First Lady. Being in the Governor's Mansion gave Jameson a preview of what life for the next few years would entail. It might be on a vastly smaller scale, but there were similarities. Leading the State of New York was no menial task. Candace had been on-call twenty-four hours a day. She'd been navigating political minefields, the press, consoling families after tragedies made by nature and by man for more than two years. There were times each of Candace's kids tested her patience. The same held true for Candace. There were moments when she and Candace challenged each other. At the end of every day, Jameson remained grateful for those momentary upheavals. It kept her grounded and it reminded her of what mattered most. "You don't need to explain it," she told Marion. "Not at all."

"I have this strange feeling that today's lunch is about more than a photo-op," Candace offered.

President Wallace nodded. "What have you surmised from the security briefings?"

"How long do we have?"

"Touché."

"It might help if you pointed me in the direction you want me to travel."

"Rusnac."

"Is there something new that I am unaware of?"

"What if I told you that Rusnac had met with Ansel?"

"Phillipe Ansel?" Candace asked.

"That would be the one—yes."

Candace sighed. "What would Ansel want from Rusnac?"

The president grinned. *That's the right question.* He was relieved that Candace was stepping into the Oval Office. He'd learned throughout his time in this building that asking the right questions was half the battle in solving issues. "That's the billion-dollar question," he replied.

Phillipe Ansel was a part of the Nationalist Front in France. The party was still reeling from its setback in recent elections. Ansel was thought to be the new leader of the party. He maintained an anti-immigration stance, was widely considered racist and homophobic, and made clear his commitment to setting a new course for France; a course that would turn back the clock on globalism and civil rights.

"It's no secret that Rusnac wanted Wolfe to be sitting here," Candace said.

"No," Wallace agreed. "But we both know that someone is pulling his strings. He's not a general. He's a foot soldier."

"Any ideas?" Candace inquired.

"Too many. That's the problem. There's a shift, Candy. It's more than backlash."

Candace considered the president's assessment. She understood that with progress came backlash. No matter how arduous the task was at securing equal rights, no matter how many decades fights were waged, setbacks endured, and small victories won; it always seemed that when a major battle ended it had occurred overnight. It unsettled people.

Globalism carried enormous opportunity for every nation. It also added to the complexity of governing. Shifting from national economies to worldwide enterprise had resulted in economic hardship for many workers in every country. Some nations had become more adept at handling the fallout, at creating new avenues for development and employment. A million factors impacted outcomes. Countries like the United States were faced with layers of intricacies — population, ethnic, racial, and religious diversity, and geological differences all conspired to create regional culture. Some regions of the country had prospered from globalism and technological advancement. Others had grown stagnant. Economic hardship fueled bias of any and every kind.

Candace had experienced the wave of both liberalism and conservatism during her campaign. Change produced passionate responses in people. She'd listened to many of her supporters' pleas for stronger and more affordable healthcare and education, often comparing the success of Scandinavian countries and much of Western Europe in securing national healthcare and education to America's perceived failings. European nations appeared to be more accepting of diversity and able to provide for their citizens. To some degree, that was true. Candace always listened. She agreed with the goal. She also understood the enormity of the task. America was vast in space, diverse in ways most people did not take the time to examine, and had an enormous population to provide for. The grass was always greener on the other side of an ocean. That's what she'd come to understand. Just as America was facing a tide of anti-immigration sentiment, revitalized racist rhetoric, movements to turn back the clock on women's and LGBT rights. Most of America's European allies were fighting to hold back the same surge.

Candace allowed her mind to roll through a series of questions and thoughts before responding. "How much do we know about Ansel's travels?"

Wallace grinned. Candace was astute. "Not as much as I would like."

"That's why I'm here," she guessed.

"Whatever I set in motion will fall to you," the president replied.

Candace nodded her understanding.

"I can give you my thoughts," he said. "My recommendation. I will put the final decision in your hands."

"I don't expect you to…"

Wallace held up his hand. "In just about five weeks, you will be sitting where I am. It will take time for any operation to take shape. We both know that. The best chance there is for success demands that you hold the reins from the get-go."

"I appreciate that."

"We've come a long way, Candy. We're standing on a tall ledge and we both know it. There are people who want to wall off our desire to build a bridge across it."

"I know. What are you thinking?"

"I think we need strategic partnerships. I think that you are uniquely positioned to secure those."

Candace understood the president's meaning. *Jane Merrow.* She nodded. "There are risks," she said.

"There are always risks."

"Yes, there are. Off the books?"

Wallace smiled. "Sometimes, that's the only way."

Candace sighed inwardly. She was not above going off the grid to keep the nation secure. It was not her preference. "What makes you think it's the only way?"

The president moved behind his desk and pulled out a bottle of scotch.

"That bad?" Candace joked.

"It's that kind of conversation," he said.

Candace accepted a glass and took a small sip. "I'm listening."

"Turning back the clock is more than a pipe dream. There's a movement in Germany, Denmark, the UK, Belgium, even in Canada."

"I'm aware."

"Yes, but the money is flowing freely. The issue is pinning the sources of the money. The FBI has had no less than twenty open investigations for the last two years targeting campaign finance, money laundering, and human trafficking; all of them pointing to this unholy alliance that has taken shape. Not one of those investigations has determined the head of the snake. The State Department has open investigations, the ATF, the DOD, not to mention NSA. Foot soldiers—that's all we've got. Beyond the obvious stakeholders in Russia, Ukraine, and China, the question remains open. Who is pulling the strings in the West?"

"I'll make some calls," Candace said. "I'd like that initiative to coincide with something official."

Wallace grinned. Candace Reid might as well already be sitting in his seat.

"What?" Candace asked.

"You're ready," he said.

"I hope so."

"Don't question it," he advised. "You are. I'll put a plan to paper with State, Defense, and the attorney general."

"Good."

"Candy," the president began.

"Yes?"

"This — what we are talking about; it is the single most powerful influence on everything you hope to accomplish — everything."

Candace nodded. Influence. Whoever held the greatest influence created the narrative. Whoever created the narrative ultimately succeeded in accomplishing their goals. "Then I suppose I need to assume the role of Persuader in Chief as well."

Wallace raised his glass. *I think you've already got that one covered.*

CHAPTER FOUR

DECEMBER 20TH

"Momma!"

Jameson snickered. Cooper was a ball of excitement. She and Candace were set to travel back to New York in a couple of days. Jameson didn't blame Cooper. She missed home as well. She missed their family. She had to admit that she had been surprised by how well Cooper had adjusted to his new school. And, Jameson hadn't expected to enjoy living in the DC area as much as she did. Candace was busy; late nights and early mornings were the norms. Despite hectic schedules and pressing issues that demanded Candace's attention, it seemed to Jameson that they had found more quality time to spend together with Cooper. As much as she missed all of Candace's kids and their grandchildren, Jameson was grateful to have an opportunity to concentrate on their marriage and Cooper.

"Ready to see Spencer?" Jameson guessed.

Cooper nodded excitedly. "Momma?"

"Yes?"

"Do we still have company tonight?"

Jameson smiled. "In fact, we do." She laughed when Cooper pumped his fist in the air and ran off.

"Where is Cooper off to?" Candace asked.

"Who knows? Probably to plan for Dylan."

Candace chuckled. She was looking forward to the evening. Alex and Cassidy were set to arrive sometime in the late afternoon and planned to spend the night. Jane Merrow would join them for dinner. Cooper loved Dylan Toles. Dylan was his hero. Cooper's excitement was an added bonus to the visit.

"I imagine you'll be working with Cassidy late tonight," Jameson said.

Candace shook her head. "Actually, I was hoping you wouldn't mind spending some time with Cass and the kids."

Jameson's curiosity was piqued. She'd assumed that aside from a chance to visit with friends, Alex and Cassidy's visit had been arranged for Candace and Cassidy to consult on the inaugural address.

Candace sighed. "Cass and I speak daily."

"Yeah, I know. What's going on?" Candace asked.

"Nothing you need to worry about."

"Candace, anything that concerns you is something I need to worry about."

Candace smiled. "I appreciate that. I'm serious."

"Please tell me there isn't some psychotic stalker targeting you."

I'm sure there is. There always is. "None that have been brought to my attention."

"That makes me feel better."

"Alex and Jane have experience in areas that I don't. You know that."

"Did something come up in your security briefing?"

"Something always comes up in those briefings. That doesn't mean there's an inevitable outcome."

"But there is an inevitable threat," Jameson guessed.

"There are all kinds of threats," Candace replied honestly. "Most of them don't involve the types of weapons you're imagining."

"And, you think Alex and Jane might be able to shed some light?"

"I think that I need to keep the people I trust close and in the loop when I can."

Jameson nodded. "I get it; let it go, JD."

"No. I can't tell you something I don't know, Jameson. And, the truth is the more I learn, the less I know."

"Kind of like parenting, huh?"

Candace laughed. "You could say that."

"Promise me one thing—just one thing."

"If I can."

"If it is ever about a threat to you, you will tell me."

"I promise."

"I'm serious."

"Jameson, I promise."

"Good. So, I get Cass and the kids?"

"Think you can handle it?"

Jameson shrugged. "Just Dylan?"

Candace grinned.

"Oh no… Mackenzie too?" Jameson guessed.

Candace let Jameson sweat for a minute. Mackenzie was Alex and Cassidy's second child. She was one of the most intelligent children Candace had ever met. She was insatiably curious and not afraid to speak her mind. She adored Jameson. More accurately, she enjoyed the fact that she could successfully torture Jameson with endless questions. "Not this trip," Candace said. "Cass is bringing Fallon."

"Babies I can handle," Jameson said.

Candace laughed and kissed Jameson on the cheek. "Yes, you can."

"Hey, Candace?"

"Hum?"

"Do you think Cass would want to play some pool?"

"From what I understand she's pretty good. You might want to rethink challenging her."

"It's just a friendly game. We can play with the kids."

Candace shrugged. "Just make sure you pick Dylan for your team," she advised.

Jameson's brow furrowed. *How good can she be?*

Alex leaned back in her chair and sipped the bottle of beer Candace had liberated from Jameson's stash for her. "You said you had some questions."

"I have more than *some* questions. It seems all I have lately are questions," Candace admitted.

"Care to elaborate?" Jane asked.

"Phillipe Ansel," Candace said.

"What about him?" Alex asked.

"That's the question," Candace replied.

"He's close to the Russian inner-circle," Jane offered.

"I assumed. He's been meeting with Rusnac," Candace explained.

"For what purpose?" Alex asked.

"I don't know," Candace said. "From what President Wallace shared with me, tracking his movements has become somewhat problematic of late."

Jane looked at Alex, took a breath and turned her attention back to Candace. "You want us to put something in motion," she surmised.

Candace nodded.

"At the FBI?" Alex asked.

"No," Candace responded. "I want you to keep your ears open at the FBI, though."

Alex pinched the bridge of her nose.

"Is that a problem?" Candace asked.

"It's not a problem. It'd be easier with a different director at the helm."

Candace's gaze narrowed with her unspoken question.

Jane offered an explanation. "Director Lansing isn't Alex's biggest fan."

"Why is that?" Candace wanted to know.

"Hard to say," Alex offered. "My past?"

"You mean your time at the CIA?" Candace asked.

"Partly. Look, Candace, there are always agents working off the books at the bureau; trust me on that. It helps if you have someone looking out for you."

"You still report to AD Bower?" Candace wondered.

"Yes."

"What's your read on Lansing?" Candace asked Alex.

"I'm not sure I have one. He's been throwing dirt in our path," Alex said.

"Dirt?" Candace asked.

"Junk cases," Alex clarified. "Cases rookies could solve easily. Not the kind of cases agents like me or Claire are suited for."

Candace's fingertip stroked her bottom lip as she considered the information. "He was President Strickland's appointment."

"He was," Jane said.

"His tenure is up next year," Candace said, more to herself than to the room. She contemplated the situation silently for a moment. "Who would you put there?" Candace asked Alex.

"Me?"

"Yes, you," Candace replied.

"Candace, I'm not a politician. Appointments are political," Alex offered.

"I'm not asking for a political assessment. I'm asking for your appraisal of what that position entails and who is best qualified to occupy that role."

"I don't know," Alex said. "Usually, the director had prosecutorial experience. That's not my expertise."

"But, you work hand in hand with prosecutors."

"Yes…"

"Okay," Candace went on. "Who jumps to mind? More importantly, who would you *trust*?"

Alex sighed. Who did she trust? Trust was a precious commodity in Alex's line of work. She cared for many people. She enjoyed friendships with people. The circle of trust in Alex's life was comparatively small. "I trust the people in this room," Alex said.

"Somehow, Alex, I don't see any of us stepping into the FBI as its director," Candace offered. "Unless, of course, you're entering your application now."

"Me? No thanks."

Candace chuckled. "Then who?"

"Rebecca Troy," Alex replied.

Candace leaned back in her chair. Rebecca Troy had served within the Justice Department for nearly twenty years. Candace recalled her confirmation as US State's Attorney for the District of Columbia vividly. Troy was considered intelligent, thorough, and a Pitbull in the courtroom. She'd read a few of Rebecca Troy's closing arguments and was familiar with a number of the cases Troy had successfully tried. "Why Troy?"

"She asks the right questions," Alex said. "She has an investigator's brain. She doesn't look for easy convictions. She's determined to get it right—not just get someone."

"And, Lansing?"

"Tired," Alex said. "Bitter. I don't know. He's interested in numbers, Candace, not justice."

"And, if Troy were the director? Would that create a more favorable environment for what I am requesting?"

"Hard to say. I don't know Rebecca that well. My sense is that she's loyal to her job, not to the person who put her in it."

"Let the chips fall as they will?" Candace asked.

"Something like that, yes," Alex replied.

Candace turned to Jane. "What do you think?"

"Rebecca Troy doesn't have any alliances in my world that I'm aware of. She was appointed when John was in office," Jane recalled.

"I remember," Candace said. "Look, Lansing's number is up. It's up in a year. That doesn't mean I can't make a change before that."

"Candace, like I said, I'm no politician, but aren't you worried that people will think this is over the top?"

"No," Candace said. "I'll admit, making a change immediately wasn't on my radar. Ansel is only a link," she said. "We know he's linked to Rusnac, and I know that Rusnac helped line Lawson Klein's pockets."

"And Bradley Wolfe's," Jane interjected.

"Yes," Candace said. "National security entails more than preventing ground wars, missile launches, and terrorist attacks. We all know that. There are a million ways to effectively render us paralyzed, and too many vulnerabilities our adversaries can exploit. We all know that there are entities within this government who aren't only willing, but who would be eager to help — whether it's for financial gain or some sick sense of power. I know what I'm asking. I wouldn't ask if I believed I had another alternative."

"What about the appearance of," Alex began.

Candace shrugged. "Someone will always take issue with everything I do. That's nothing new. Changing straight away makes sense. It allows me to start with a seamless team."

"Ask Tate his opinion," Alex suggested.

Candace nodded. "Alex, I won't hold it against you if you refuse. I know that you intended to leave that life behind."

Alex sighed. She'd accepted a role back at the FBI reluctantly a year earlier, after five years away from investigative work. She'd held positions at the DOD, NSA, and CIA during her career. One thing Alex did know, the world was a dangerous place. Thankfully, most people lived in blissful unawareness of the threats that loomed daily. She'd hoped that stepping away might secure her family's safety. If only it could. Cassidy often reminded Alex that safety was an illusion. The best anyone could do to protect the people they loved was to be present and honest, and to do their best at whatever they did best. Alex was best at solving puzzles. "Tell me this much," Alex requested.

"I'll tell you whatever I can," Candace promised.

"How important is this to you?" Alex asked.

"It's not about me, Alex. It's about us—all of us. Progress is painful. It doesn't come without upheaval. You know that as well as I do. Progress as you and I see it, that type of progress means evening the playing field. Not everyone wants to compete on a level field. Some people prefer to stay atop the hills they've enjoyed for eons. That means relegating someone else to the valleys below. Those people will always exist. They are the wall builders. We are the bridge builders. There is no me, and there is no you. That's their narrative. What I am asking you to do isn't for me; it's for us."

Alex nodded her understanding.

"What about Claire?" Candace asked.

"I trust Claire with my life. She'll be on board," Alex promised.

Candace looked at Jane.

"You have me at your disposal. You do realize what you are suggesting we create?" Jane asked Candace.

Candace nodded. "I do."

"Then count me in," Jane said.

"Good."

⚘

Jameson shook her head in disbelief.

Cassidy laughed. "Alex should have warned you."

"Candace tried," Jameson confessed. "Where did you learn to play?"

"Alex," Cassidy said. "She gave me lessons." Cassidy smirked.

"Ah." Jameson chuckled.

"Even I can't beat her," Dylan said. "Mom has a competitive side."

"Not really," Cassidy dismissed the thought.

"Yeah, right." Dylan laughed. "Did you know that Mom almost became an Olympic skier?"

"You're kidding," Jameson said.

"He is," Cassidy replied.

"Am not. You could have," Dylan said.

"In my experience, if you could have; you would have," Cassidy commented.

"You could have," Dylan said. "She's still amazing on the slopes," he told Jameson.

Cassidy rolled her eyes. "Still? Are you implying I'm old?"

"Not old, just *older*," Dylan teased.

Cassidy laughed. "Can't argue with that." She picked Fallon up from her portable crib. "Why don't you give Cooper a lesson down here?"

"Sure," Dylan said. "What do you say, Coop?"

"Yeah!" Cooper jumped up and down.

"Twist his arm; why don't you?" Jameson laughed. "We'll be upstairs if you need us," she told Dylan.

"Me and Coop will be fine," Dylan promised.

"Feel like a beer?" Jameson asked Cassidy.

"I would love one."

"I hope Dylan is okay entertaining Cooper."

"It'll break him in for tomorrow when we get home. He'll have three Coopers vying for his attention."

"You sure do have your hands full," Jameson said. "I don't know how you do it. I don't know how Candace did it all those years."

"What's that?" Cassidy asked.

"Raise kids and work."

"I don't really work," Cassidy said.

"That's not how Candace tells it."

"Candace is generous. I love helping her. I only help; believe me."

"I think you help more than you realize." Jameson reached into the refrigerator and pulled out two bottles of beer. "So? Any idea what this visit is all about or should I not ask?"

Cassidy jostled Fallon on her hip, accepted a beer and shrugged. "I don't know. Do you want my best guess?"

"Please."

"I would imagine Candace is hoping Alex and Jane have some information she needs. That, or she's hoping they'll help her get the information she needs."

Jameson nodded.

"Worried about her?" Cassidy guessed.

"It's not like I didn't know we were walking into a hornet's nest," Jameson confessed. "Maybe it's just becoming real. Don't get me wrong; I wouldn't change it. Candace is meant to do this. At least, I think she is."

"She is."

"It's strange; you know? To me, she's Candace. I see what everyone else sees in her, but she's my wife. It's hard sometimes to remember she's about to become the leader of the free world. Sometimes, I wonder how I ended up here."

Cassidy smiled. "I understand."

"Somehow, I thought you might."

Cassidy followed Jameson into the living room and took a seat on the sofa. "Life throws us some insane curveballs," she said.

"No joke." Jameson chuckled. "I never imagined myself married or a mom, much less married to the president-elect."

Cassidy winked. "I know it isn't easy, JD."

"What do you mean?"

"Well, people like Candace and Alex, they thrive living in the broader world. They can say that's not true, but it's who they are."

Cassidy had hit the proverbial nail on the head. Candace often protested her need to continue up the political ladder, to be immersed in the world's problems, and to solve them. That part of Candace's world was as much a part of who she was as being a mom or wife could ever be. Jameson accepted that.

"They're different from us," Cassidy offered. "People think that Candace and I are alike."

"You are," Jameson said.

"In some ways. Just like you and Alex are alike in some ways. But, JD, I think the truth is you and I are more similar."

"You do?"

"I do. I don't need that world. I see it. I know it exists. I know that the world requires people like Alex and Candace. Alex is always telling me that I should think about doing something more for myself — professionally."

"Sounds familiar."

"I'll bet it does. She has some crazy idea that I gave something up to have our family, to allow her to follow her path."

"That sounds familiar too."

Cassidy chuckled. "It's not that I don't find it all fascinating; I do. I didn't sacrifice anything. She's my path; if that makes sense. I have what I've always wanted. It's more than enough for me."

Jameson sipped her beer thoughtfully. "Can I tell you something?"

"I hope so."

"I never thought about having a family until I met Candace."

"And now?"

The weight of the truth fell on Jameson as she began to speak. "And now, it's the only thing that matters to me, Cassidy. Candace, the kids—I know a time will come when I will go back to work. It'll come in time. I don't know what that will look like. I don't think about it. I think about…"

"What?" Cassidy urged gently.

"Sometimes, I think about what I missed with all of them. I wish we could have had it all together."

"Mmm. In that way, you are just like Alex."

"What do you mean?"

"Well, Alex missed the first six years of Dylan's life. I think they both mourn that at times. He sees her with Kenzie or the twins; she sees Fallon do something, and they both wish they could have that memory of each other."

Jameson nodded.

"Have you ever thought about it?" Cassidy wondered.

"What?"

"Having a baby with Candace?" Cassidy asked.

Jameson closed her eyes. She had. "I have."

"Does she know?"

"No."

"Why not?" Cassidy asked.

"I know that's not what's best for us," Jameson said. "I do know that. We have Coop and I'm so grateful for that every day."

"I can imagine."

"But we missed time with him too."

"It's not easy," Cassidy said.

"No, but I wouldn't change any of it."

"I think I understand."

"I'm glad she has you," Jameson said.

"Me?"

"Yeah. She trusts you, Cassidy. She feels like she can talk to you about the things she might not want to share with anyone else. You're her best friend; you know that; don't you?"

Cassidy smiled. She and Candace had grown incredibly close over the last two years. They spoke daily, and their conversations covered far more topics than public appearances or political issues. Children, wives, aging parents, hopes, fears, dreams — they confided in each other about all of it. Cassidy knew what was in Candace's heart when it came to both her career and her family. She was grateful for the way their friendship had grown. And, she was aware that Candace felt the same way.

"Well, I will tell you something," Cassidy said.

"What's that?"

"If there is anything that you are holding back from Candace—don't."

Jameson sighed.

"Don't," Cassidy repeated. "I learned that the hard way with Alex. Tell her, JD. She loves you."

"I know."

"She can handle it, and she wants you to tell her. Alex and I, we've made that misstep a few times—held something back. It always backfires in the end."

Jameson appreciated Cassidy's candor. She told Candace almost everything. She'd said nothing about the fact that her biological clock suddenly seemed to be knocking at her brain.

"It's normal, JD," Cassidy said. "What you're feeling; it's normal. It doesn't mean it'll lead to anything more than a conversation. Tell her anyway."

Jameson sighed. *I'll think about it.*

⁂

"You've been quiet," Candace observed.

Jameson nestled closer to her wife. "I had a long talk with Cassidy."

Candace ran her fingers through Jameson's hair. "A good talk?"

"I think so."

"Want to share?"

"Candace?"

"Hum?"

"When you… When you…"

"When I what?"

"When you hit forty did you start thinking about kids?"

Candace pulled Jameson a little closer. *Ah, the truth comes out.* "I did."

"Really? You already had three."

"You have four and you're thinking about it," Candace said.

"Not exactly. I didn't give birth to any of them." Jameson sighed. "Do you think it's strange?"

"That you find yourself thinking about having a baby? No."

"But I never thought about it," Jameson said. "Ever. Not ever."

"Things change sometimes."

"You're not upset?"

Candace shifted so she could look at Jameson. "Upset? Honey, why on earth would you think that?"

"Because. Because I know that's not something you want. We agreed."

"Jameson, are you trying to tell me you want to try to have a baby?"

"No," Jameson said. "I'm not."

"But?"

"But part of me wonders if I'll regret that I didn't."

Candace kissed Jameson's lips tenderly. "I told you a long time ago that if that's what you wanted, I would be open to it."

"Why am I so confused?"

"Because our life is upside down right now," Candace said. "And, because you are feeling the gravity of time."

"Maybe."

"Jameson, you can tell me anything."

"Yeah, I know. I just... I can't imagine going through that. And, you have so much on your plate. It's just... watching Shell and now... I don't know. Don't you think Marianne and Scott will try to have a baby?"

"Probably."

Jameson sighed. "What's wrong with me?"

"Nothing is wrong with you."

Jameson placed her head on Candace's breast. "I wouldn't be thinking about it if we weren't together."

"I wouldn't be so sure of that."

"No, I don't think so. And, Candace? I'm not saying it *is* something I want. I feel like I've been hiding the truth from you."

Candace kissed Jameson's temple. "Sweetheart, no offense, you can't hide much from me."

"You knew?"

"I suspected you were wrestling with it; yes."

"Why didn't you say something?" Jameson wondered.

"Because I knew you would when you were ready."

Jameson let out a sigh of relief.

"Feel better?"

"I do," Jameson confessed. "I don't think it's something I want to do but I can't help that I wonder about it."

"No, you can't. You can talk to me about anything. Don't forget that."

"I know. It's just this is something that…"

"It's something that's on your mind. That makes it something that matters to me," Candace said. "I realize that having a baby isn't something you've yearned to do. And, I know that you've been reluctant to tell me what you're feeling because of all the change."

"It's not just that."

"And, because we've discussed this before."

"Exactly."

"Jameson, life changes sometimes. People grow, not just our kids; we grow too. There are a lot of things I am unsure about. The one thing I am certain of in my life is you. Don't forget that. There isn't anything on this earth you couldn't ask me for. That much I can promise you."

"I love you; you know?"

"Of course, I know. I love you too."

Jameson took the first deep breath she had in weeks. Everything she'd told Candace was true. She had been thinking about her ticking biological clock.

Would she regret never having a child? Did she want to share that with Candace? Would she look back and wonder what might have been someday? Her feelings were ill-timed. Maybe it was all the gentle teasing from Shell and Jonah about her joining the baby club. It was more than that, and Jameson knew it. It was about her love for Candace. It was about Cooper and how much she reveled in being his mother. It was all of it, and as hard as Jameson tried, she'd been unable to banish her thoughts and feelings on the subject. Knowing that Candace understood relieved the weight she'd been carrying for weeks. She decided to shift topics. "How was your talk with Alex and Jane?"

"Productive."

"Is that good?"

"I certainly hope so," Candace said. "Time will tell."

"You'll figure it out. You always do."

I hope so, Jameson; for all our sakes; I hope so.

CHAPTER FIVE

DECEMBER 24TH

"Are you happy to be home?" Marianne asked her mother.

"You have no idea," Candace said.

"Only a few more weeks, Mom."

"I know." Candace poured herself a cup of coffee.

"You don't sound particularly happy about that," Marianne observed.

"It's not that."

"What is it?"

"It's nothing."

"Mom?"

"There are a million things to do, Marianne. I'm not sure I've given Jameson the time that she deserves lately."

"She understands."

"She might understand, that doesn't mean it's okay."

"Are you worried about JD?"

"Not worried — aware."

"I'm missing something," Marianne said.

"There's a lot of change happening for her right now, Marianne."

"I can imagine."

"I'm not just talking about the move or my work."

Marianne sipped from her mug. She enjoyed a close relationship with Jameson. In fact, she would say that Jameson was her best friend. She'd spent two hours the previous evening catching up with her stepmother. She hadn't detected that anything was bothering Jameson. Something was clearly on her mother's mind. "You don't have to tell me anything," she said. "Whatever you tell me, stays with me," Marianne promised.

Candace reached over and squeezed her daughter's hand. "I know that." She sighed. "I just hope that your brother and sister give her a little break on the teasing while we're home."

"You know Shell, she delights in getting a rise out of JD."

"Yes, I do. But some things might hurt a little more than Shell takes the time to think about."

"What things?"

Candace sighed.

"Mom? Seriously, I spent a long time with JD last night. What is this about?"

"Marianne, Jameson is not getting younger."

"Jameson's forty-one. That's hardly old."

"No, it isn't. She'll be forty-two this year."

"So?"

Candace sighed again.

"Oh. Oh, shit. JD's biological alarm clock just sounded."

"Something like that."

"Can't say I saw that coming."

Candace smiled.

"You did?"

"She's my wife, Marianne."

Marianne nodded. "Does she want to try?"

Candace shook her head. "I don't know."

"What did she say?"

"What she always says; it's not something she's ever desired."

"Until now."

Candace chuckled. *Oh, I'm not sure I'd say that.* "That's what she would say."

"And, you? How do you feel about it?"

"Honestly?"

"Yes."

Candace sucked in a long, deep breath. "It scares me."

Marianne nodded.

"I'm not sure what scares me more, the idea that she'll tell me she wants to or the fact that she likely won't want to."

Marianne smiled. Her mother's revelation didn't surprise her. "Maybe you should tell her that."

"Maybe I should," Candace agreed. "I think she needs some time right now to sit with everything."

"And you?"

"I told you how I feel."

"Well, that would certainly get tongues wagging."

Candace laughed. "Because they aren't tied up enough in our business."

Marianne shrugged. "Well, selfishly; I wish you two would consider it."

"Really?"

"I know. I know. Things change, Mom. I love JD."

"I know you do."

"She's my best friend." Marianne grew emotional.

"I know she is," Candace said. "She feels the same way."

"She's a terrific mom."

"Yes, she is."

"So are you. I'll admit, I thought any chance of that ended when you got elected."

Candace smiled.

"You didn't?"

"I told you; she's my wife, Marianne. I know Jameson."

"Cooper would be deliriously happy."

Candace laughed. "Probably so."

"Why is Cooper going to be deliriously happy?" Michelle asked. She strolled through the kitchen and poured herself a cup of coffee.

"Hello, to you too, Shell," Candace said.

"Hi, Mom."

Marianne rolled her eyes.

"Where are the twins?" Candace asked.

"JD has them."

"Both of them?" Candace asked.

"Yeah, why?" Michelle asked.

Marianne chuckled and arched a brow at her mother.

Candace laughed. "I'll go give her a hand."

"Why?" Michelle asked again. "You know, JD; she's a kid magnet. If she had any sense, she'd jump on the wagon with the rest of us."

Candace's expression hardened.

"What did I say?" Michelle asked.

"Leave it be, Shell," Candace advised as she left the room.

"What did I say?" Michelle asked her sister.

"Just go easy on teasing JD about babies the next few days," Marianne offered.

"Why? Oh my God, is she knocked up and they didn't tell us?"

"Shell," Marianne warned. "I'm serious. Lay off. It might be fun for you. It might not be so much fun for JD."

Michelle flopped into a kitchen chair. "What's going on? Are Mom and JD fighting or something?"

"No."

"Well? What gives? JD knows I'm just giving her a hard time."

"Shell, please trust me this time. Please don't go there this Christmas."

Michelle studied her older sister. "Is JD sick?"

"Not that I'm aware of." *Although, your questions could make anyone dizzy.*

"Well, something is up."

"Nothing is *up*, Shell. I'm asking you. Mom is asking you; please leave it be for a while."

Michelle was confused. She and Jameson's relationship had always involved gentle teasing and banter. She loved Jameson. Jameson knew that. Jameson loved her. Michelle knew that. All of sudden, her teasing was an issue. "You're not making sense," she said.

"Only in your brain," Marianne said. She sighed. *Shit.* "Listen, I think JD has enough on her mind right now without you giving her a hard time about having kids. That's all."

Michelle held her hands up in surrender. "Okay. I'll find something else to harass her about."

Marianne shook her head. "I have no doubt."

༄༅

Jameson bounced Brody on her knee while she listened to Cooper and Spencer running up the stairs. *It never gets old.* "What do you think, Brody?" Brody giggled. "I don't know either," Jameson said. "Your cousin and your uncle are nuts; just like the rest of this crazy family." He laughed some more. Jameson caught sight of Candace approaching and kissed him on the head. "Don't look now," she whispered to her grandson. "The head lunatic is on her way."

"Dare I ask what you two are discussing?" Candace teased.

"Asylums," Jameson said.

"Ah. Well, that's certainly a topic we have some knowledge of."

Jameson chuckled. "I'm glad that Shell decided to stay tonight."

"Mmm. So, you can steal the twins and play with them?" Candace guessed.

"I don't know. It feels strange without Jonah here tonight."

"They'll be here in the morning."

"Yeah, I know."

"Are you worried about talking to him?" Candace asked.

Jameson sighed. She and Candace were planning to talk to Jonah and Laura about taking over their town-home in Virginia once Candace took office. Was she nervous? She was hopeful that they would accept.

"If it helps, I think they will both be excited at the possibility," Candace said.

"I hope so. You know Jonah. He's proud, Candace. He might see it as a handout."

"It won't be a handout if he rents it."

"Do you think he'd want to do that?"

"I think he is more apt to be open to your idea if he contributes."

Jameson sighed again.

"He wants you to be proud of him, Jameson."

"I am proud of him."

"I know you are."

Brody grabbed a fistful of Jameson's hair. "Ouch." Brody laughed.

"Anything to get a reaction," Jameson said. "Just like your mother."

Candace giggled. *Truer words.* "Speaking of Shell, where did she and Mel disappear to?"

"Not sure where Shell is. Mel took Amanda upstairs to put her down," Jameson offered.

"Maybe she's with Marianne," Candace mused.

"Nope. Don't think so. Marianne went upstairs to give Maddie a bath."

"Huh."

"Worried she might be up to something?" Jameson asked.

"Shell is always up to something," Candace said.

Jameson laughed. "That's for sure. Maybe she's snooping in the attic for presents."

"God help us all." Candace let herself recline on the sofa. She put her head on Jameson's shoulder. "He's gotten so big. I feel like he's grown in a couple of weeks," she said.

"He has," Jameson agreed. "What are your mommies feeding you?"

Brody erupted in a belly laugh.

"Why do they all laugh at me?" Jameson wondered aloud. "Am I that funny looking?" Jameson asked.

Brody laughed harder.

"I am?"

Candace shook her head. "You certainly are in your element, honey."

"I'm not sure if that's a compliment or an insult."

Candace kissed Jameson on the cheek and let her head fall back onto its resting place. *It's definitely a compliment.*

"What's up?" Michelle asked Scott.

Scott drew patterns in the condensation on his beer bottle.

"It can't be that bad," Michelle said.

Scott offered Michelle a half-hearted smile. "I bought Marianne a ring."

"That *is* awful." Michelle laughed. "Why so glum?"

"I'm not sure if I should give it to her."

"Lost me."

Scott took a long pull from the bottle in his hand. "Maybe I should wait. This is your mom's time."

"What the hell are you talking about?"

"Exactly what I said. This is your mom's time. It's only a month until her inauguration. I don't want to complicate anything or seem like I'm... I don't know, stealing anyone's thunder."

"Did your mom drop you when you were a baby or something?"

"What?"

"I'm serious," Michelle said. "Do you know my mom?"

"I..."

"Do you think Mom worries about that stuff?"

"No, but it's amazing and I..."

Michelle shook her head. "Are you afraid Marianne will say no?"

"Not really."

"Then what is the problem?"

"I told you."

"I call bullshit," Michelle said. "If you want to propose to Marianne, I think you should."

"On Christmas morning?"

"Is that what you want to do?" Michelle asked.

"I want to propose."

"Are you asking my advice or am I here to get you drunk?"

Scott chuckled. "Both?"

"Fair." Michelle took a deep breath. "If you want my advice, don't ask her in front of everyone."

Scott nodded sadly.

"Ask her. Don't make it a display. Ask her tonight or ask her in the morning before you come down with the kids."

"I kind of hoped the kids could be part of it."

"Sweet." Michelle smiled. "I get it. I would make this one personal, Scott. It might seem like I am the family fuck up."

"Shell..."

"No, listen; I know Marianne better than most people realize. If you don't believe me; ask JD. She'll tell you what I just did. She'll also tell you not to make Mom an excuse to chicken out."

Scott took another swig of beer.

"She's not going to say no," Michelle said. "She loves your sorry ass for some reason."

Scott laughed. "Thanks for the endorsement."

"We all love your sorry ass." Michelle put an arm around her sister's boyfriend. "I hope you know what you're signing up for."

"You mean having a mother-in-law in the White House?"

"Nope. I mean dealing with me and Jonah."

"Do your worst," Scott said. "If she says yes."

"Oh, she will, and you'll wish you never gave us permission to initiate you."

"You mean I haven't already been initiated?"

"Nope. Drink up," Michelle advised.

Scott complied. "Do you think JD has more beer?"

"Liquid courage? I'd wait to polish off her stash until Marianne agrees."

Scott groaned.

"Out of curiosity, why didn't you talk to JD?"

"You're not serious. She'd probably threaten my life."

Michelle nodded. Jameson had given Melanie a gentle warning when she and Melanie had started dating. "Eh, she's not so bad. Just… if you hurt Marianne make sure you stay away from JD when she's got a hammer or a saw or a…"

"I've got it."

Michelle laughed. "Welcome to the family."

"I hope so."

Now, I get to tease Marianne about the baby club!

⚜

"Nana?" Spencer looked at Candace.

"Yes, sweetheart?"

"What if Santa misses us?"

"Santa knows where to find you," Candace promised.

"But, Mommy, what if he thinks me and Spence are somewhere else?" Cooper asked.

Candace took a seat on the edge of Cooper's bed, which he and Spencer had decided to share for the night. "What did Momma tell you?"

"Santa is magic," Cooper said.

"Jay Jay says Santa just knows stuff," Spencer offered.

Candace bit the inside of her lip to keep from laughing.

"He does," Jameson said from the doorway.

"But how?" Cooper asked.

"Santa has cookie radar," Jameson said.

Cooper and Spencer's eyes grew wider. Candace bit the inside of her lip again.

"What about the reindeer?" Spencer asked.

"Carrot radar," Jameson offered.

"They'll find us, Spence! We put out the carrots," Cooper said.

Candace glanced over at Jameson leaning in the doorway. Love and gratefulness filled her. These moments reminded Candace of the things that mattered most to her. She cared for the world's plight. She felt compelled to ease suffering where she could. She was dedicated to becoming a president that would strive to lead everyone forward. She felt pride, humility, awe, gravity and excitement about her future. At this moment, the expression of wonder in her son's and grandson's eyes, the affection and amusement that poured off Jameson — nothing could ever compare to the way it made Candace feel — nothing.

Jameson noted the affectionate sparkle in Candace's eyes. She made her way across the room and put her hand on Candace's shoulder. "There is a clause, though," she said.

"Like Santa Claus?" Spencer asked innocently.

"Well, it's called the Santa Clause—with an 'e.' You have to be asleep for the radar to work," Jameson told the boys.

Cooper burrowed underneath the covers and pulled Spencer down beside him. "Come on, Spence! You heard Momma."

Spencer snuggled under the blanket with his best friend. "Nana?"

"Yes, Spencer?"

"Do you know Santa?"

Candace grinned. "We've met," she told him.

"Mommy! You met Santa?" Cooper jumped back up.

Candace laughed. "You met him last week."

"Nah," Cooper said. "He was Santa's friend. Santa's too busy to visit everyone."

"Oh?" Candace asked.

"Yeah. His beard was fake. Momma told me."

Candace reached up and squeezed Jameson's hand. *God, I love you, Jameson.* "Momma knows a lot about Christmas."

"Yep," Cooper agreed.

"Maybe Jay Jay is an elf," Spencer offered.

Jameson coughed.

"Are you, Momma?" Cooper asked. "Are you one of Santa's helpers?"

Candace thought her heart might burst. Inaugurations be damned. Maybe Jameson was an elf. She certainly possessed magic. At least, Candace thought so, and she was positive the boys agreed. "Momma has a little magic," Candace said.

Jameson cleared her throat. "Okay. I'm not on Santa's payroll. I do know that he needs the whole house to be snoring before he'll come down the chimney."

"But there's a fire, Jay Jay!" Spencer said.

"I'll make sure the fire is out," Jameson promised.

"He'll get dirty," Cooper said.

"Nah," Jameson dismissed the thought. "He's got magic laundry detergent too."

Candace chuckled. *Magic laundry detergent?*

"Like for the washer?" Cooper asked.

"Sort of. You know that stick Mommy carries in her bag? That Magic Eraser thing?" Jameson asked.

Candace covered her eyes.

"Yeah?" Cooper said.

"That's Santa's invention. He's got a super big one."

"Okay, I think we can all rest now," Candace said. She needed to end the conversation before she lost all hope of controlling herself. She was sure once she started laughing, she'd never stop. She leaned over and kissed Cooper, then Spencer. "Goodnight."

"Night, Nana."

"I love you," Cooper said.

"I love you too," Candace promised.

"Night," Jameson said.

"Jay Jay?" Spencer called after her.

"Yeah, Spence?"

"Maybe we can leave Nana's eraser. Just in case," Spencer suggested.

Candace had to turn away.

Jameson felt Candace's body shake with laughter. "I'll find it," she said.

"Put it with his cookie!" Cooper called out.

Jameson nodded as Candace pulled her through the door.

"What's so funny?" Jameson asked.

Candace couldn't speak. She couldn't recall the last time she'd laughed this hard.

"What?" Jameson said. "I had to think of something."

Candace wrapped her arms around Jameson's neck and kissed her deeply.

"Mm... I didn't know how much you loved those eraser things."

"Stop it." Candace laughed some more. "I love you, you lunatic."

"Yeah? Enough to help me put that crazy train set together that you bought Coop?"

"Enough to get you beers while you do it."

Jameson kissed Candace gently. "Sounds like the perfect partnership."

"Yes, it does."

꩜

Jameson let her head fall back against the sofa and closed her eyes. She'd finished Cooper's train in record time and opted to sit on the floor against the sofa. Candace had taken up residence between Jameson's legs. Jameson enjoyed the warmth of Candace's body pressed against hers. Her hands met in front of Candace's stomach and she sighed.

"Tired?" Candace asked.

"Relaxed."

Marianne walked into the room and smiled. "Did all those cookies you ate give you a sugar coma?"

"I love your mom's cookies," Jameson said.

"There's tomorrow's headline," Michelle said.

"Isn't it past your bedtime?" Jameson asked.

"No. Might be past yours, though. Don't you get a bedtime again after forty?" Michelle teased.

Marianne glared at her sister.

"What? You never said I couldn't give her shit about her age," Michelle said.

Jameson opened one eye. *Oh, boy.*

Marianne made no reply.

"Actually, I'm pretty tired," Melanie offered.

"You want to go to bed *now*?" Michelle asked her wife. "Before we get to watch Scott muddle through the directions for that castle he bought Maddie?"

"Unless it has a bed that fits my fat ass, I'm going upstairs," Melanie said.

"You're not fat, babe," Michelle's eyes sparkled. "Not yet, anyway."

Jameson opened both eyes. *No way.*

"Shell?" Marianne asked.

"Yeah, well... See, here's the thing. We thought it would take, you know, a while.... Like maybe a year or so, if it worked... So, we thought if we wanted the kids to be two years apart, we should start," Michelle started to explain. "Didn't expect first-time to be the charm. Guess they'll be more like a year apart instead."

Candace pulled herself from Jameson's grip and embraced Michelle, then Melanie. "You must be over the moon," she said to her daughter-in-law.

"More like terrified," Melanie confessed.

Candace smiled compassionately. "I'm sure all will be well."

"I hope so," Melanie said.

Michelle took her wife's hand. "It will be. At least, you don't have to deliver two."

"There is that," Melanie agreed.

Jameson followed Candace's lead and hugged Michelle and Melanie. "Congratulations," she said. "I know how much you hoped this would happen," she told Melanie.

"Thanks, JD."

Jameson nodded. She felt Candace's hand slips into hers and give a tender squeeze.

Marianne watched the scene unfold with interest. She wasn't surprised by Michelle and Melanie's news. She expected that any baby news from Michelle would occur in a more distant future.

"Well, this is it for us," Michelle said. "Three's company."

"And, four's a crowd?" Jameson asked.

Marianne looked at Jameson. Cooper made four in their family.

Michelle shrugged. "I take it back. Maybe when I get to your age, we'll add another."

"What?" Melanie asked.

"Sure. Space them out like Mom and JD. Why not? This bunch will be in school. Round two?"

Melanie shook her head. "I wish I could ask for a drink."

Candace laughed. "How many months of sobriety do you have left to endure?"

Melanie grinned. "About seven."

"Umm... More than seven," Michelle said. "You're not pumping IPA."

"I'm not pumping at all," Melanie said. "That's your obsession."

Michelle grumbled. "We'll see."

Melanie rolled her eyes. "Since I can't drink, I'm going to bed. Goodnight."

"Night, Mel," Marianne said.

Jameson caught Melanie by the arm. "Hey..."

Melanie smiled.

"I'm happy for you, Mel," Jameson said.

"Thanks, JD. I'll feel better about it in another month or so."

Jameson nodded.

"Guess that's my cue," Michelle said. "Wait up, Preggers."

Candace rolled her eyes. "Does she ever stop?"

"No," Marianne offered.

Scott chose that moment to descend the stairs.

"Where did you go?" Jameson asked. "Lose the instructions or something?"

"Or something," he said.

Jameson was curious. *What is he up to?*

"Are you ready to head up?" Candace asked Jameson.

"Whenever you are."

"I am."

"Guess that leaves you two crazy kids," Jameson said. "We'll see you in the morning." She took Candace's hand and started toward the stairs. "Oh, wait!"

"What?" Candace startled a bit.

Jameson held up a finger and jogged out of the room.

"What is that about?" Marianne asked.

"I have no idea," Candace confessed.

Jameson jogged back into the room and held up the eraser pen Candace's carried in case of mishaps. She placed it next to the plate of cookies on the mantle.

"I'm not going to ask," Marianne commented.

Candace grinned and held out her hand for Jameson. "Goodnight," she said. "We'll see you in the morning."

"Night Mom. Night JD," Marianne replied.

"Don't drink all my beer," Jameson told Scott.

Scott looked like a deer caught in headlights. "Me? No worries, JD."

He is up to something. Jameson nodded and let Candace lead her away.

Candace looked at Jameson curiously when they reached the top of the stairs. "Are you okay?"

"Me? Yeah, why?"

"Just making sure."

"Did you think Scott was acting weird?" Jameson asked.

"Weird? No."

Jameson shook her head. "He's up to something."

"Maybe he's just eager to have a little time alone with Marianne."

"It's something else," Jameson surmised.

Candace tugged on Jameson's hand. "I don't want to talk about the kids—any of them."

"No?"

"No."

"What do you want to do?"

Candace smirked. "I thought you could show me some of your elf tricks."

Jameson wiggled her eyebrows. "Looking for a little magic, Mrs. Reid?"

Candace pulled Jameson into their bedroom and shut the door.

"Anything in particular you'd like to see?"

Candace cupped Jameson's breast in her palm and placed her lips a whisper from Jameson's. "I hear elves can close their eyes and transport anywhere."

"Mmm."

"How does that work?"

Jameson's hand found the back of Candace's neck. "I'll show you."

Candace accepted Jameson's kiss gratefully. *Definitely magic.*

꿈᛭꿈

Marianne watched as Scott shifted nervously in his chair. "What is wrong with you?" She giggled.

"Nothing; why?"

"You're squirming like Maddie does when she has to pee."

"I'm not squirming."

Marianne arched an eyebrow exactly as her mother did when she issued a gentle challenge.

Scott scratched his brow. "Can you come over here?"

Marianne's gaze narrowed. "I'm right here."

"Yeah, but can you come over *here*?"

Marianne shrugged and crossed the room. "I think maybe you and JD ate too many cookies."

Scott took a deep breath for courage and dropped to his knee.

Marianne's jaw dropped.

"I've never done this, so I hope I do it right," he said. He took another breath and met Marianne's watery gaze. "I know that I can never replace what you lost. And, before you stop me; I think that's important for me to say. I love you, Marianne. I love being with you. I love sleeping beside you. I love Spencer and Maddie. I love what we have together. I don't want to wake up without you beside me anymore. I want to be the one to take Spencer to soccer and I want to be the one to sit with Maddie when she's not feeling well. I want to be the person you fall asleep beside every night. I want to spend my life with you and with your family. So..." Scott steadied his breathing and opened the box in his hand. "Will you marry me, Marianne?"

Marianne dropped to her knees in front of Scott and took his face in her hands. "Yes, I will," she said, and kissed him tenderly.

"Thank God."

Marianne laughed. "You don't need to replace anything or anyone," she said. "I love you for you. Don't forget that."

He nodded.

"And, Scott?"

"Yeah?"

"You are my family."

Scott pulled Marianne close and kissed her again. "Merry Christmas."

"Merry Christmas, honey."

CHAPTER SIX

"I can't believe Mel is pregnant," Jonah said.

Jameson smiled.

"Holy shit! Is that why you and Mom want to talk to us? Are you two…"

"No," Candace put the thought to rest and held Jameson's hand.

"Oh." Jonah's voice dripped with disappointment.

"Sorry to disappoint you," Jameson said.

"Nah. I just thought maybe… Never mind. What did you want to talk to us about?"

"How much more thought have you put in to opening an office in DC?" Jameson asked.

"Some. I don't know, JD. It'd make sense. The thing is; I thought Shell would jump at moving. With Mel expecting, I don't see that happening now. Bryan is great as a negotiator, but as an architect… I just don't know who we would place there to oversee things."

"What about you?" Jameson suggested.

"Me?"

"Why not you?" Jameson asked.

"I'm not an architect."

"No, but you understand the concepts as an engineer and you know how to select talent."

"JD?" Laura looked at Candace and Jameson. "We'd have to find someplace to live and. "

Candace held up a hand. "We thought you might be interested in taking over the townhouse."

"Your townhouse?" Jonah asked.

"Well, it would be *your* townhouse if you wanted," Jameson said.

"JD, you and Mom have already helped us too much."

"You can't help your kids too much," Jameson said.

Candace smiled and let Jameson continue.

"Listen, you and Mel are in charge at the firm. It's yours to run. I've noticed all the travel you've had this year. One of you is always on the road, and most of the time you are in Maryland, Delaware, DC, or Virginia. An office makes sense." She sighed. "And, to be honest, I'd like it if you were closer to us."

Jonah grinned. He missed his mother and Jameson. Laura missed Candace. He knew that too. "I can't accept a freebie."

"No freebies. You rent the townhome. If you want to buy it, whatever you pay in rent will be your down payment," Jameson said.

Candace looked at Laura. "I thought you might consider helping with some social outreach projects I have planned."

"Me?" Laura was surprised.

"Why not you?" Candace asked.

"I don't know…"

"Well, you don't have to decide today. Jameson and I would love it if you accepted. We'll understand if you don't."

Jonah looked at Laura and immediately knew the answer. "We don't need to think about it."

"Which means?" Jameson asked.

"I could use your help, JD. Hiring staff, I mean. I know you can't insert yourself. If you could review the applicants or..."

"I'd be happy to."

"Good, then that's settled," Candace said.

"Mom?" Jonah called for Candace's attention.

"Hum?"

"There's something that I wanted to talk to you about too."

"We're listening," Candace said.

Jonah took a deep breath. "I don't want you to say anything at all, okay? Just listen before you say anything."

Candace and Jameson both nodded.

"Okay... We've been talking. I know... Well, I know that you and JD don't want kids—I mean besides us and Coop."

Candace's brow furrowed. *Where is this going?*

"And, I get that. I just... Well, Coop said something the other day when you got home and..."

"What did Cooper say?" Jameson asked.

"Just that he heard you crying in the kitchen with Grandma."

Candace felt as though she'd been punched in the gut. She had no idea that Jameson was hurting that much.

"Crying?" Jameson asked.

"He said he heard you say something about never having kids with Mom."

Jameson groaned. "I wasn't crying," she explained. She looked at Candace. "I wasn't. I was sneezing." She laughed. "I swear."

Candace let out a sigh of relief.

"I was talking to Pearl," she explained. "Before she left to visit Jeffrey. Was Cooper upset?"

"No, I don't think so. He heard Grandma tell you that you still had time for babies."

Jameson massaged her brow. This conversation made her uncomfortable. She'd never intended to tell anyone about her feelings. All of a sudden, the entire world seemed to know? It left her feeling vulnerable and embarrassed. "We were just talking," she said.

Jonah nodded. "Yeah... Well, listen... As weird as this might sound; if you did—if you and Mom wanted to; I would be happy to try and help."

Jameson's jaw dropped. "Jonah..."

"Hey, I'm not offering anything old-fashioned."

Candace couldn't help herself. She laughed. She was shocked by the turn their conversation had taken, and the look on Jameson's face relieved her tension.

"Okay. I have had enough baby talk," Jameson said.

"JD," Jonah grew serious again. "I mean it. I get it. You don't want to talk to us about it. And, I get that you'll probably never ask. I just want you to know that you can."

Jameson forced herself not to cry. "Thanks."

Jonah found his feet and took Laura's hand. "Do you care if I raid your beer?"

Jameson shook her head.

Candace waited for her son and daughter-in-law to leave. "Are you okay?"

"Not even a little bit."

"He loves you, Jameson."

"Yeah…"

"Jameson." Candace turned Jameson to face her. "Maybe we should talk about this subject a little more."

"What subject?"

"You talked to Pearl."

"I made a comment in passing and Pearl lectured me."

"And, you talked to Cassidy."

"It came up in context, Candace."

Candace nodded. "I didn't say we should have a baby, Jameson. I said that maybe we need to talk about how you feel about it more."

"I don't know how I feel about it. I know how you feel about it. And, I don't have time to figure it all out."

"You know how *I* feel about it?" Candace asked.

"I think so."

Candace shook her head. "Jameson, the idea of babies scares the hell out of me. I'm almost sixty-two. That is not an age people generally start families. That doesn't even scratch the surface of what I'm about to walk into."

"I told you; this is my issue to stare down. I don't know why it's even on my mind so much. I told you that."

"But it is," Candace said. "For the record? There is a big part of me that wishes you would tell me you want that."

Jameson sat shell-shocked.

Candace grinned. "I love you. I love raising Cooper with you. Don't you think I wonder about it too? We've been through this, honey. I was thrilled for Shell last night. I felt that little tug too, the one that reminds me how much I wish we had shared that—all of it."

Jameson let her head fall onto Candace's shoulder. "I never expected to feel like this."

"I know. It's okay."

"You said something to Shell; didn't you?"

"No. I just told her to lay off on her teasing."

Jameson sighed. "I don't want people walking on eggshells with me."

Candace placed a kiss on Jameson's cheek. "I have something for you."

"What? We already exchanged gifts."

"You can consider it executive privilege." Candace walked behind her desk and retrieved a box.

"What is it?"

Candace laughed. "I guess elves don't have x-ray vision. Open it."

Jameson tore the wrapping from the box and lifted the cover. She smiled at the contents. "Candace…"

"Who knew I was such a great photographer?"

Jameson lifted the framed photo from the box and let her eyes sweep over the faces behind the glass. Candace had snapped it at the annual Fourth of July party. Jameson was sitting by the pool with Cooper, Spencer, Maddie, and JJ. "Thank you."

"Thank you," Candace said. "You are an amazing parent, Jameson. I don't ever want you to doubt how much this family loves you and needs you — not just me — all of us."

Jameson pulled Candace down and kissed her. "I need you too."

"Well, then I guess it works out for all of us."

"I guess so."

Candace held out her hand. "What do you say we go see who's running the asylum?"

"That's easy."

"Oh?"

"Yeah. Shell thinks she is. Marianne lets her think it."

Candace laughed. "Probably accurate. What do you think about Scott and Marianne?"

"About time, I'd say." She walked hand in hand with Candace. "I'm happy. I still miss him, though."

"Rick?"

Jameson nodded.

"Me too," Candace said. "Me too."

Jameson stopped Candace.

"What?"

Jameson kissed her in reply. "Merry Christmas," Jameson whispered. "Next year we'll have a few more trees to decorate."

"And, a few more hands to help," Candace said.

Jameson smiled. "Good thing we're moving into a bigger house."

🎀

DECEMBER 31ST

Marianne sipped her glass of wine thoughtfully. Jameson had been quiet all evening. She wondered what was on her friend's mind. "Want to talk about it?"

"I was just thinking that you'd probably be moving soon."

"Soon?" Marianne shook her head. "We're not getting married tomorrow."

"No, but I would imagine that you and Scott will be staying at his house."

"Actually, I was hoping maybe you and Mom would be okay with us living here until you come home."

Jameson was surprised.

"Unless that's a problem," Marianne said.

"Of course not."

"Scott's place is small for four people. That's why Shell sold it."

"Even smaller when it becomes five."

"That's not happening any time soon," Marianne said. "I'm not ready for that just yet. I think we need some time to be a family first before we add to that."

"Aren't you already?"

"Yes, but you know as well as I do that living with someone changes things."

"Can't argue with that."

"When it's meant to happen, it will happen," Marianne said.

Jameson nodded.

"Are you ready to head back to Washington?"

"Define ready," Jameson replied.

"Nervous?" Marianne inquired.

"Not really." It surprised Jameson that she felt little anxiety about living in the White House. Home would be wherever Candace and Cooper were. She loved the house in Schoharie. For Candace and Jameson, this place would always feel the most like home. It's where they had fallen in love. It's where Candace had spent the happiest times of her childhood. Priceless memories were attached to every nook and cranny of the old house. Familiar, friendly ghosts greeted you at every turn. "I'll miss this place."

"I don't blame you," Marianne said. "I will too when the time comes. So, make sure Mom gets two terms."

Jameson laughed. "I'll let her know how you feel."

"JD?"

"Yeah?"

"Do you think Pearl will be okay? I mean, with Mom being so far away all the time?"

Jameson wasn't sure how to answer that question. Candace had spent long weeks in Washington when she was in the Senate. She was home most weekends. This had been home. That was about to change. "I've thought about that."

"Yeah."

"I thought I'd suggest that Pearl come with us."

"You're serious."

"Why not? The third floor is ours to use. There's more than enough room for her to have space. And, honestly, Marianne? I think it'd be good for both of us. I worry about Coop when we travel without him. He's used to having you or Pearl nearby."

Marianne understood.

"You look sad," Jameson said.

"Cooper..."

"You and Coop have a special bond."

"Like Spencer with you," Marianne said. "I'd be lying if I told you part of me hoped Mom would lose."

Jameson listened without comment. Marianne's admission didn't surprise her. When she and Candace had first started their relationship, Jameson would never have dreamed that Marianne would become the closest to them as a couple. Rick's death had devastated everyone. If there was any purpose to the loss, Jameson believed it had been the relationship she shared with Marianne now.

"I can't imagine not seeing Coop," Marianne said. "Or you."

"You know, you can come visit any time," Jameson said.

"I know. We both know that won't be as often as we'd like."

"For what it's worth, I will miss you too."

Marianne smiled. "There's something I wanted to talk to you about."

Jameson held her breath. *At least, she won't be offering me sperm.*

"Are you okay?" Marianne asked.

"Yeah, I was just thinking about something Jonah said. What's up?"

"When we set a date — me and Scott, that is," Marianne hesitated.

"Yeah? You want to get married on the South Lawn?" Jameson teased.

"No, thank you." Marianne laughed.

"The Oval Office?"

"I'll leave that one to you and Mom."

Jameson grinned evilly.

"You are a little touched, JD. Forget I said that."

Jameson laughed. "Okay, so no White House weddings."

"Not that white house anyway." *Oh, just tell her.* "I was wondering if, when the time comes, if you would be willing to stand up for me."

Jameson was speechless.

"Uh, JD?"

"I would love to. I just thought you'd ask Shell."

"Well, the truth is; I think Scott will want you to stand with him," Marianne confessed. "And, if that happens, I will ask Mom. But I needed you to know that I want you there. I know we don't say it much; you really are my best friend, JD. I don't think I would have survived Rick's death without you and Mom."

"You would have."

"Maybe. I'm glad I didn't have to."

"Me too."

"Are you really going to ask Pearl to move to DC?"

"That depends on your mom."

"You haven't said anything to her?"

"Not yet. I thought I'd bring it up tonight."

"What do you think she'll say?"

"I don't know," Jameson admitted. "I guess, we'll see."

Candace rocked Amanda in her arms. Shell's twins were as different as they were alike. Brody seemed to be able to fall asleep amid chaos and noise. Amanda needed to be comforted to rest. Brody was already independent at the tender age of seven-months-old. He could entertain himself and everyone else in the room. In more ways than Candace could count, Brody reminded her of Shell. Amanda preferred the closeness of another person. Not that Candace objected, she reveled in the ability to hold her grandchildren. Amanda, much like Spencer, had gravitated to her Nana immediately. If Candace was in the room, the infant sought her embrace. Candace cooed to the infant and Amanda smiled.

"She doesn't want anyone but Candace when we're here, not even you," Melanie commented to Jameson.

Jameson smiled. "Babies aren't that different from adults in a lot of ways."

"You mean that eventually, we all need someone to change our diapers?" Michelle joked.

"I guess that does even the playing field. No, I meant that babies are people. They fit with certain people the same way we do," Jameson offered.

"Uh-huh. Maybe. I've always thought Spencer was like your own personal growth," Michelle said.

Jameson grinned.

Melanie rolled her eyes. "Gross, Shell."

"What? The moment he laid eyes on JD, he forgot about the rest of us," Michelle said.

"That's not true," Jameson said. "He's still his Nana's boy." She looked over to see Cooper and Spencer hovering over Candace. "See?"

"Yeah, I know. I think all the kids would live with you two if we let them."

Jameson laughed. "That's because we're the grand-parents," she said. "We get to bandage all the boo-boos and play with them."

"And, Coop?" Michelle asked.

Jameson beamed. "Cooper jumps at every chance he gets to sleep at one of your houses. It's just the way it goes, Shell. They don't love us more, just differently."

"I guess," Michelle commented. She shrugged and made her way over to Jonah.

"JD?" Melanie began.

"Yeah?"

"Feel like a walk?"

"A walk?"

"Just to the kitchen."

"No wine for you," Jameson said.

"Ha-ha, I was thinking a change of scenery."

Jameson nodded. She could easily understand a need to escape the quiet rumble in the living room.

"I was kind of surprised that you wanted us all here on New Year's Eve," Melanie said as they walked.

"It's our last hoorah before the inauguration," Jameson explained. "When we head back to DC, it'll be complete chaos for three weeks. After that? I think it'll be a while before we get back here for any amount of time."

"I'd say I can imagine, but I can't."

Jameson laughed. "It's a bit surreal — the whole thing. Candace has meetings all day, every single day when we get back. Cassidy's coming up next Friday to work on the speech with her."

Melanie nodded. "You don't look happy about that."

"What? No," Jameson said. "It's not that at all. I have meetings all that week too."

"Really?"

"I have to hire a staff."

"You've done that before," Melanie said.

"Yeah, of architects and engineers, not social secretaries and politicos."

"Candace can help."

"She can. She's so busy, Mel. I want to be able to handle it. I need to be able to keep this off her plate."

"What about Dana?" Melanie asked.

Jameson sighed. "Becoming Press Secretary is nothing to sneeze at. She's got her hands full."

Melanie considered Jameson's situation. "Why don't you ask Shell to come down for a week or so?"

"Shell?"

"Why not Shell? You worked together on the campaign. She'd love it."

"I think you and Shell have enough to deal with."

Melanie shrugged off Jameson's assessment. "You mean because we're having a baby or is it because Jonah is going to relocate?"

"Both."

"Well, neither is happening in the next month, JD."

Jameson groaned. She was hesitant to ask for Michelle's help. It was one of the reasons she hadn't said much to Candace about the anxiety she felt in hiring staff and setting her agenda as First Lady. Candace would likely make the same suggestion. The last thing that Jameson desired was to add any stress to Michelle and Melanie's life. They had seven-month-old twins, Melanie had plenty to handle at the architectural firm, and now, Melanie was pregnant. That added another wrinkle.

"You'd be doing me a favor," Melanie said with a chuckle.

"A favor?"

"I love Shell more than anything. She's bored out of her mind, JD. Shell is a great mom. She needs more than bottles and diapers to fill her days."

Jameson sighed. "What about you?"

"Me?"

"You'll have three sooner than you think. What about your career? I mean, Mel, three little ones?"

"I'm not leaving the firm, JD. I will have to pull back on travel. I know that complicates things with Jonah looking to open a second office, but..."

"Family first, Mel."

"Yeah. Shell and I aren't built to be stay at home moms. We have to find a balance between us. I think Shell would like to be home more than she wants to be away from the kids. She needs something for herself too. Helping you in some capacity—JD, I think that might be the ticket. She misses you a lot."

"She misses her mom and the campaign trail."

Melanie shook her head. "Yes, but she misses *you* too."

Jameson was confused.

"JD, you and Shell used to be the best of friends."

"What do you mean, used to be?"

"I just mean that you've become closer to Marianne and Jonah than you were once. I think sometimes Shell feels a bit like she's been relegated to playing second fiddle."

Jameson's heart dropped rapidly. Shell meant the world to Jameson. They'd bonded immediately. "That's not true at all."

"I know that," Melanie said. "Think about it, though. When you and Shell were first friends, Marianne was in Texas and you two were still bumping heads. Shell was *your* protector."

True.

"Jonah was still at school in California," Melanie reminded Jameson. "You hadn't gotten a chance to get to know him yet."

"Yeah, but..."

"I'm just saying that things have changed," Melanie explained.

"I love Shell."

Melanie smiled. "I know you do. I remember having my life threatened when we started dating."

Jameson sniggered. "That's a bit of a stretch."

"Maybe, but trust me; I know how much you care about her. She loved spending time with you during the election. It meant a lot to her, JD. You know Shell; she's not one to express her feelings the way Jonah or Marianne will. She shows it by teasing you endlessly."

Jameson sighed. She'd been surprised when Melanie and Michelle had started seeing each other. She was protective of Shell. Their friendship was something she treasured. Jameson had always thought of Michelle a bit like a younger sister; a younger, annoying sister who she would walk through fire for over and over again. But Shell was more than that. She was also Jameson's step-daughter, and Jameson would do anything to keep her family safe and happy. Taking a moment to think about it, she hadn't made much one-on-one time for Shell for a while. She shook her head regretfully.

"Hey, JD... Shell knows you love her. I just think she misses you. You two were inseparable once."

"Are you sure you would be okay with me asking? I'd need her in DC during the week, at least a few days for the next month or two."

Melanie grinned. "Totally okay. Laura is still here. Marianne is here if I need anything, JD. Ask Shell. I think it might be what you both need right now."

Jameson nodded. *Maybe it is.*

⌇⌇

"You disappeared for a while," Candace commented.

"What do you think about me asking Shell to help with setting up my office in the White House?"

Candace grinned. "I think it would be good for both of you."

"Maybe."

"Is there some reason you don't want to ask?"

"Truthfully?"

Candace nodded.

"I feel kind of funny. If I'd known about Mel's pregnancy, I might have reconsidered suggesting Jonah make the move to DC."

"I see."

"You disagree?" Jameson wondered.

"I wouldn't say that. Jameson, the kids might be kids to me, but they're adults — capable adults — all of them."

"I know that."

"I would be willing to bet that Shell is driving Melanie insane."

Jameson was curious. "Why? Did Mel say something to you?"

"No, but Shell was droning on and on about Melanie slowing down."

"Oh, boy."

Candace grinned. "You know how Shell is. She talks a good game."

"If she's worried, what makes you think she'll accept my offer?"

"She loves the twins, Jameson. She's bored."

"That's what Mel said."

"Shell has always needed a million moving parts to keep her sane. She came out of the womb that way." Candace chuckled. "Jonah was content to play by himself or to sit with a single task for hours. Marianne, well, you know Marianne."

Jameson laughed.

"Shell? Shell's interests have always been endless. She has so much energy. She needs to put it all somewhere. And, if you want to know the truth, I think she's struggling with what she wants to do."

"What do you mean?" Jameson asked.

"She feels guilty for being away from the twins, but she needs an outlet. Finding a balance isn't easy."

"Speaking from experience?"

"I am." Candace fluffed the pillow behind her head and pulled Jameson close. "I felt guilty whenever I had to leave them. I still do."

"I know." Jameson did know. She didn't need any visions of the past to understand that Candace often felt torn. She saw it daily with Cooper. Candace and Cooper loved each other so much it sometimes took Jameson's breath away to watch them together. There were many nights when Candace came home from a long day at work or on the campaign trail and sat on the edge of Cooper's bed watching him sleep. Jameson felt Candace's inner battle. She was sure that it had been the same with The Three Stooges.

"Sometimes, I wonder if I would do it all the same way again," Candace confessed.

"You would."

Candace smiled. She would. That was the truth. It was strange when she thought about it. She knew that her path had not been to be at home with her children all day, each day. She tried to be present when it mattered. She carved out quality time for all her children; at least, she did her best to make time. She would put anything aside if one of them needed her. But Candace needs more than a homemaker's life. She'd always felt a modicum of guilt over that reality. She admired Pearl. Pearl had spent a lifetime nurturing her family, Candace included. Candace could barely recall a milestone that Pearl hadn't been present for. Pearl had bandaged almost every scraped knee, dried Candace's tears after a broken heart, listened to Candace's dreams and comforted her after nightmares. Pearl had done that with each of Candace's children and grandchildren. Part of

Candace wished she could find contentment in that life. And, part of her feared she'd failed in some way as a parent because she couldn't.

"Candace?" Jameson shifted to look at her wife. Candace's eyes seemed distant. Jameson smiled. "I know what you're thinking."

"You do?"

"Yes, I do. You're feeling guilty about Cooper and about the kids."

Candace sighed. "Sometimes, Jameson, I wonder if it was fair of me to want them so badly when I had so many other things I wanted to do."

"I know. Not one of the kids feels that way."

Candace sighed.

"Candace, they don't. Listen to me for a minute."

"I'm listening."

"Look at you."

"Me?" Candace questioned.

"Yes, you. Your mom was home all the time."

"My mother never longed to have children."

"How do you know that?" Jameson asked.

"Jameson, you know how my mother was."

"I do, but maybe part of that was because she never felt she could have other things too. I don't know. I'm just saying that being home all the time doesn't make someone a better parent."

"Maybe. I can't help that I wonder."

"I think I understand that."

Candace nodded. "Melanie's pregnancy got you thinking some more."

"It did. Not the way you might imagine."

"Care to share?"

Jameson sat up and took a deep breath. "I think that part of me is always going to wish we had that together, Candace — a baby."

Candace listened. *Me too.*

"But I don't think that's our path."

Candace nodded.

"You look disappointed."

"I am," Candace said. "That doesn't mean I don't agree. Jameson, I love you so much. How could I not wonder about that?"

Jameson smiled, leaned over, and kissed Candace sweetly. "There are so many people right now that we both want to give to. Cooper needs the time we have to give."

"Yes, he does."

"And, Candace? I could never love any baby more than I love Coop."

Candace smiled. Cooper meant the world to them both. He'd given them something that neither had expected to share. He was the light of their lives. "Neither could I."

"That's what I mean. He needs us. The kids need us. As much as I know I will always look back from time to time and wonder, I think we need to focus on the family we have. I don't think it's done growing," Jameson said.

"Safe bet."

"And, Candace?"

"Yes?"

"Remember when we first talked about this? Back when Marianne had me knocked up before we'd even gotten engaged?"

Candace sniggered. "I seem to have a vague recollection of that, yes."

"Do you remember what I told you?"

"I do."

"I have to share you with the entire world. I don't think I want to split any more time than I have to."

Candace held Jameson's face in her hands. "Are you sure about this?"

Jameson nodded. "I can't tell you it doesn't hurt a little."

"You don't have to tell me. I already know."

"When Mel and I were talking, she told me she thinks Shell misses me."

Candace grinned.

"You think so too?" Jameson asked.

"She does," Candace said.

"Did she say something? Because Mel seems to think my relationship with Marianne and Jonah has changed things."

"It has," Candace said.

Jameson sighed and closed her eyes.

"Jameson, that isn't something to feel badly about."

"Have I been blowing off Shell?"

"No," Candace said. "I think sometimes she misses the way it was when we were first together. She didn't have to compete with Marianne and Jonah for our attention—for your attention."

Jameson sighed again. "Fuck."

Candace chuckled. "It's not easy balancing everything and everyone."

"No. I need to focus on the family we have, Candace."

Candace kissed Jameson in reply. "Thank you."

"For?"

"For reminding me why I love you so much."

"Candace, if you want..."

"What I want? Jameson, I have more than anyone has a right to enjoy, much less want. Sometimes, I worry that I will let you all down."

"Never."

"I hope you're right."

"Candace, we love you because of who you are."

"And, we love you because of who *you* are. You are an incredible mother, and not just to Cooper."

"I'm not..."

"In every way that matters you are. I couldn't do this without you—not this. I wouldn't be where I am, Jameson. I don't mean the presidency. I mean my life. I've told you this before; I need you to know that I mean it. If you come to me tomorrow and tell me that you've changed your mind, about having children, I will move heaven and earth to make it happen."

Jameson smiled. Candace's voice carried both emotion and resolve. "I know you will. I won't change my mind." She fell into Candace's arms. "So, you're okay with me asking Shell?"

"More than okay. And, Jameson?"

"Yeah?"

"You can ask me for help too."

"You have enough…"

"Nothing takes precedence over you in my life."

"There is something else I wanted to talk to you about."

"What's that?" Candace asked.

"Pearl."

"Pearl?"

Jameson sat up and took a deep breath. "What would you think about asking her to come with us to Washington?"

Candace stared at Jameson with disbelief.

"Bad idea?" Jameson asked.

Candace couldn't seem to form any words.

"I have to say, this is not the reaction I expected."

"Of all the things I might imagine you wanting to discuss, that was nowhere on the list."

"There's a list?" Jameson attempted to lighten the mood.

Candace sighed. "Jameson, I don't know if Pearl…"

"You won't know if you don't ask."

"Pearl's entire life has been here, Jameson. I can't imagine she'd want to change that now."

Jameson considered her reply before speaking. Pearl missed Candace sorely. Candace was a confident woman. Confidence didn't mean that Candace never needed encouragement. Pearl understood Candace in ways that no one else ever would, not even Jameson. Jameson could listen to Candace, hold her, make love to her, make her laugh, and support her as a wife. When things became tense between them, Pearl was Candace's rock and shoulder to cry on. Jameson understood that most people looking in had developed a fairy tale concept of her marriage to Candace. People forgot that every fairy tale had its challenges — moments of doubt and darkness. She loved Candace more than life itself. Love did not equate to perfection. The pace of their lives, the number of people competing for their attention, even their age difference at times caused friction. No one's life and no relationship existed without some turmoil. Working through those periods is what gave the happy times the most meaning. Jameson had come to understand that since meeting Candace.

Candace was about to embark on a mission that carried the literal weight of the world. Jameson had a front row seat. Listening to the press, one could easily develop the idea that Candace Reid was a colorfully programmed robot; a person always in control of her feelings and her destiny. It's not that Candace hid her emotion from the public. Leading required that she exhibit assuredness, and instill a sense of calm in others in the face of crisis and tragedy. When the cameras clicked off and the door closed to their room at the end of a day, Jameson witnessed the toll it all took on her wife. Candace was not made of stone. Even stone was made of sand. Jameson thought that people lost sight of that fact. A stone was millions of grains of sand pressed together. Hit a rock hard enough and it shattered back into all those fine grains of sand. Things are not always as they appear on the surface. Jameson pondered that thought often.

"Candace," Jameson began cautiously. "You said it yourself; the kids are adults now. Pearl's boys are away. Think about it; when Jeffery is here in the states, he tends to be in DC. He has to block time to visit Pearl here in New York."

Candace's emotions were running along the surface of her being, threatening to spill over at any second. Jameson's revelation that she did not want to have a child had torn away a small part of Candace's heart. The reaction surprised her. She agreed with everything Jameson said. It still hurt. Feelings weren't rational; they simply were. She should be relieved. Some part of her was relieved. She also knew they would revisit the decision over and over throughout their lives as a couple and privately. Security briefings, staffing concerns, speeches—none of it had affected Candace as deeply as the happiness she felt hearing Melanie was expecting or the tug she felt at the realization Jameson had made a decision about having a baby. Life never stopped. It rolled along in the face of loss and upheaval. Pearl had been the steadying hand in Candace's life for nearly all of it. Would she want Pearl to move to DC? She would.

Jameson made an excellent point. Candace's kids were grown. They loved Pearl, but they had lives now that didn't require her constant presence. Pearl's younger son, Jeffery worked for The State Department. He was overseas most of the year. When he did come home, the majority of his time was spent in Washington DC. Excellent debate points, but would Pearl even consider a move?

"Maybe. If you were thinking about this, why didn't you say something before we offered Jonah and Laura the townhouse?" Candace wondered.

"I wasn't thinking that Pearl would live in the townhouse."

Candace's brow furrowed.

"I thought she could live with us."

Candace was speechless — again.

"Okay? Bad idea?"

"In the White House?"

"That's where we'll be; right?" Jameson asked lightly.

"Jameson…"

"Candace, the third floor is ours to use as we choose."

"I thought you wanted to keep that room Marion created upstairs?"

"I do. There's still plenty of room for Pearl."

"I don't know."

"Because you don't want her to live there or because you're afraid to ask?" Jameson wanted to know.

"Of course, I want her there."

"So, you're afraid to ask."

Candace sighed.

"I think it'd be good for both of you, but I think we should tell her the truth."

"Which is?"

"We need her," Jameson said.

Candace sighed again.

"We do. Coop needs some consistency. We both know he's going to miss Marianne like crazy. If I had to bet; I'd bet that he'll miss her more than he does Spencer."

Jameson's words brought a smile to Candace's face. She was incredibly grateful for the closeness Cooper and Marianne shared. Her bond with Marianne had strengthened in ways she'd never dared imagine a few years ago. She would miss all her children and her grandchildren. If Candace were honest, it would be Marianne she would miss most of all. Cooper sought either Marianne or Pearl in Candace and Jameson's absence. Pearl's presence would ease the transition for Cooper.

"That's a bit devious," Candace said.

"What?"

"Using Cooper to get Pearl to agree."

Jameson shrugged. "I'm using Pearl too."

Candace chuckled. "I don't know. I'm not sure she'll want to make that move."

"We won't know if we don't ask."

"You're serious about this?"

"Completely," Jameson said. "I think it'd be good for all of us. Change can be good sometimes."

"Yes, it can," Candace agreed.

"I assume you have a plan here?"

"Only to ask Pearl if she'll consider it."

"And, Pearl's house?"

"The kids can keep an eye on it."

Candace shook her head. "I don't know."

"The worst she can say is no, Candace."

Candace nodded.

"Do you want her to come?"

"Now that you've suggested it, more than you know."

Jameson smiled. "So? Let's talk to her." She pulled Candace into her arms. "What's meant to be will happen."

"When did you become such a fatalist?"

"I'm not—not really. Whatever happens, we'll make it work. We always find a way."

Candace closed her eyes. "Thank you."

"I love you, Candace." Jameson let her head fall onto Candace's. "I want this to be the happiest year ever for you."

Candace inhaled Jameson's scent. No one could sustain happiness forever. She knew that better than anyone. Jameson would move the heavens and battle the demons of hell to take care of Candace. What more could anyone want? "Happy New Year," she whispered. "I love you too."

CHAPTER SEVEN

JANUARY 1ST

"To what do I owe this dinner?" Pearl asked.

"Since when does Candace need an excuse to make lasagna?" Jameson asked.

"Candy makes lasagna when someone's upset, she feels guilty, or when she wants you to pay some attention to her."

Jameson rolled her eyes. "You spent too much time with 007 last week."

Pearl grinned. She'd taken to affectionately calling her son, Jeffrey, 007 because of his travels abroad. "Am I wrong?"

"That there's a conspiracy afoot with Candace's lasagna?" Jameson laughed.

"I'm not wrong. You're buttering me up for something."

"There's no butter in her lasagna. I watched her make it."

"Very funny," Pearl said. "Now, give it up; who's pregnant besides Mel?"

"No one that I know," Jameson said.

"Okay? Who is getting divorced?"

"What?" Jameson rolled her eyes. "You need to stop watching Lifetime so much."

"I like Lifetime."

"I know."

"Jameson, you are worse at hiding something than Cooper."

"What makes you think I have anything to hide?"

Pearl crossed her arms and leaned back in her chair.

Jameson sighed. She had intended to wait for Candace to return from her conference call to talk to Pearl. Pearl could sniff out a plan from a million miles away. "Fine. You have to promise not to say anything until you hear me out."

"I'm waiting."

"And, you have to know that this was my idea."

"Still waiting."

Jameson took a deep breath. "How would you feel about coming to DC with us?"

Pearl's gaze narrowed. "Last I knew, I was going to stay with you the first week you spend in that behemoth of a house you're moving into."

"Yeah, what if you didn't leave?"

Pearl held Jameson's gaze silently.

"What if you moved with us?"

"Why?"

"What do you mean; why? Why not?"

"Where did this idea come from?" Pearl asked.

Jameson decided to lay all her cards on the table. She glanced toward the doorway to ensure Candace was still in her office. "Pearl," she said. "We both want you to come. That's the truth. We also need you."

"You don't need me, Jameson."

"Yes, we do. We all do," Jameson said. "I've been over it a million times."

"It?"

Jameson sighed. "I could tell you that it would help with Cooper, and that wouldn't be a lie. It would help. I would feel better knowing you were there when we have to be away."

"But?"

"No *but*. Let's be honest; we all miss each other. Candace misses the kids. I miss the kids."

"They miss you."

"Yeah, but they all have families to take care of — marriages that demand their attention. That's life. That's the way it should be. We have that too. We also have…"

"The world to think about?" Pearl guessed.

"Something like that. I could tell you that having you in DC would help keep Candace steady. That's true too. It would mean the world to Candace to have you close. Those aren't the only reasons I'm asking."

"Go on."

"I miss my parents, Pearl. The last few months, I've felt out of balance."

"I know. It's that baby thing."

Jameson nodded. "Partly; yes, it is. I don't see that in my future. Cooper needs us more now than ever.

He's had so much change in his life already. He has to come first. We agreed on that when we decided to adopt him."

"And?"

"Having someone close that I know understands Candace and me—together; that is something we both could use. And, it would be a benefit for Coop. He needs to feel secure. No one knows us like you do, Pearl—no one."

Pearl nodded. "Jameson, you have never lived with me."

"Close enough. Besides, you'd have your space above us. You wouldn't have to be with us all the time."

"I should hope not."

"Jonah and Laura will be close. They'll both be starting new things. I know that Candace wants to involve Laura in some projects she has in mind."

"So, who am I there to babysit? The great-grandkids, the grandkids or you and Candace?"

Jameson laughed. Pearl was already on board. "Probably me and Candace."

"Sounds about right."

"I know it'd be a big move, but…"

"Is this what you really want?" Pearl asked.

"Yes," Candace answered from the doorway. She stepped inside and smiled at Pearl.

Jameson thought it wise to give the pair a moment alone. "I'm going to go let Coop know dinner is almost ready."

Candace's smile served as her thank you.

"Candy..."

"Mom, please; let me say something."

Pearl nodded.

"I won't say this with Jameson here. It rattles her more than I want it to."

"I'm listening."

"Time isn't a guarantee. We both know that. The entire last year—every part of it reminded me that you can't take time for granted. Life is unpredictable. Some mornings, I sit in my morning briefings and my heart flips upside down at the reminders I get that life can change on a dime. I come home after a couple of weeks; I see the kids and they've all grown. I listen to Cooper and Spencer; it seems like yesterday we were teaching them their colors. Now? They tell us stories worthy of publishing. It all goes by so fast. I hate missing any of it. This—stepping into this role," Candace paused and took a breath.

"Of President?"

Candace nodded. "To some people, it probably seems like a dream. For a lot of people, it's a nightmare..."

"And, for you?"

"It's real. It has to be real, and you can get lost in it. I can't get lost in it. I need people who will make certain that I don't. And, I miss you."

"I miss you too, Candy."

"It's selfish. I know it is. Jameson brought the idea to me, and I want you to accept so badly I feel like a little girl wandering into the kitchen begging you to let me stay with you."

Pearl smiled. As a child, Candace had often begged to live with Pearl. Life at home could be hard and cold. Candace had felt alone much of the time when she was with her parents. There were similarities now. Candace had Jameson. There would be many times in the coming years when Candace would find herself alone in The White House while Jameson was off making appearances without her. That was the life she'd chosen for them both. That didn't make it easy. Having a sense of home mattered for everyone. Pearl represented that.

"You'd better find someone to keep my house clean," Pearl said.

Candace's eyes filled with tears. "You'll come?"

"Someone's got to keep you from living on fortune cookies and wine."

Candace chuckled through her tears.

Pearl moved to wrap Candace in a hug. "I love you, Candy. All you had to do was ask."

Candace held onto Pearl.

"You should know, Candy; your grandparents would be proud of you."

Candace choked on her tears.

Pearl closed her eyes and reveled in her daughter's embrace. "Your mother and father would be too. I know you don't think so; they would be, sweetheart. I know I am."

Jameson wiped a tear from her eye when she stepped into the doorway. Pearl caught her gaze and winked. Jameson smiled and quietly left the room. *Thank you, Pearl.*

⚜

JANUARY 12TH

"Candace, be reasonable."

God, I hate that word. Nothing annoyed Candace more than when someone on her team told her to be "reasonable." She was always reasonable. Decisions had to be made and that always left someone unhappy or unsatisfied. She took time to review the arguments and opinions of the people in her orbit, and even of those who seemed to reside in a distant galaxy. At the end of debate and dialogue existed decision. That was her role. Once she reached the destination, she expected those closest to her to get on board. Candace held Doug Mills' gaze without comment.

"Did you hear everything that the experts said?" he asked.

"I heard them."

"I'm missing something," he replied.

You will be if you keep going down this road. "I'm not the president yet, Doug."

"You will be in less than two weeks."

"I'm aware."

"You need to be ready. What if…"

"There are no what ifs, Doug. There are probabilities and possibilities. 'If' has no possible conclusion. It's an open question."

"That's semantics."

"It is not," Candace said.

Dana cringed in her chair. Candace's patience with Doug Mills was wearing thin. Candace had fought to bring Mills on during campaign season as an adviser. He was well-versed in the major issues facing the incoming administration both domestically and globally. What he lacked was an understanding of the nuances involved in effective governing. Candace was a master in that realm. She looked beyond glaring concerns and popular ideologies for the subtle challenges and possibilities in every situation. Mills seemed convinced that Candace needed to take on immigration immediately. That she needed a big legislative win, and that failing to do so would lose her points with her base. Dana didn't need an announcement to know what was coming. Doug Mills was about to be schooled in the Candace Reid style of leadership.

"We aren't crafting legislation on immigration until the latter part of the year, Doug. If someone in Congress presents something, I will review it and offer my support or opposition. And, I will make my reasons and what I expect clear. As for pushing that legislation—no."

"You promised to address..."

"And, I will. Immigration isn't an easy fix."

"It's an area that both sides need to appear to be engaged in. That gives you leverage."

"It does."

Doug threw up his hands. "You know? Candace, you heard Tate and the Joint Chiefs yesterday. You've read The State Department's recommendations, and Treasury's. Should I go on? Every department in this government agrees that we need to tackle this problem. It will only fester the longer..."

"Sit down," Candace said firmly.

"I..."

"Sit down," Candace repeated. "First, let me make something clear; you are allowed to express your opinion. There is a time for that, and a way for it. Now, is not the time and your current method isn't working in your favor."

"I'm only saying."

"Stop speaking." Candace paced around her desk and leaned against the front of it. "There are thousands of issues that require my attention—thousands, not hundreds. Immigration is at the top of that list. That is precisely why we are not running out of the gate waving that flag." She watched as Doug's jaw began to move and raised her brow in warning. "It's too important to tackle without taking partners."

"You have partners."

"Yes, but not the partners we need. Can we pass something? Probably. Contrary to popular belief, *something* is not always better than nothing. In fact, *something* can create far more problems than nothing."

"You have moderates..."

Candace held up her hand. "Stop. Do you actually think we can solve this issue solely through legislation?"

"No, but that's..."

"You've had your say. It's my turn," Candace said. "Why do people come here, Doug?"

"What?"

"Well, you seem to think immigration is a simple fix. It's a simple question. Why do people want to come to the United States?"

"Economic opportunity."

"And?" Candace urged.

"And?"

"And, what else?"

"Freedom, prosperity."

"Mm. Textbook answer, Doug." Candace moved back behind her desk and resumed her lecture from her chair. "All true. There are other reasons—family, idealism, to escape persecution or prosecution. But you are correct. The number one reason people want to live here is that they crave opportunity."

"And?"

"And, we have people here that are struggling to find opportunity."

"You sound like you're buying into the Republican narrative," he commented.

"Do I?"

"Candace," Grant tried to step into the conversation.

Candace ignored him. "So, you think I am the Democrat's president?"

"That's not the point I'm making."

"What is your point, Doug? I think I've been clear about where I stand. I believe we need a common-sense pathway for people already living here to gain legal status, whether that's citizenship or resident-alien status."

"And, there are…"

"I said, it's my turn to speak," she cautioned.

Doug felt his face flush. He'd watched Candace get frustrated. She seemed to be teetering on the edge of anger.

Dana took a deep breath. Candace rarely lost her temper. The president-elect was close to blowing her top.

Candace steadied her breathing. She still had three meetings to endure before she would be able to take a break. Cassidy was due that evening to spend the weekend working on Candace's Inaugural Address. She had thought they would engage in a working dinner. That plan had just changed. She needed a break and she needed a friend. If she survived the next few minutes without killing or firing Doug, she would wade through the next three hours looking forward to sharing a bottle of wine and venting to her best friend.

"When I take the Oath of Office, I will promise to serve *all* the people of this country, not only the ones who colored in a bubble next to my name."

"I know…"

"Doug," Candace raised her voice. "Enough. Do I think that immigrants are responsible for the majority of people facing unemployment or underemployment? No. Do people believe that? Some do, and whether you and I like that fact, it matters to those people. Immigration reform has to go hand in hand with economic stimulus. That's number one. Number two: we need to address foreign policy issues. There are reasons so many people to our south seek to cross our borders. Economic depression is at the core. We have to engage with Mexico, Central and South America on trade and development. We have to create opportunity — real opportunity here and abroad. Why do you think there is a backlash, Doug? You can answer that."

Dana hid her face and snickered. She loved to watch Candace at work, explaining an issue to an intelligent, educated person as if they were a kindergartner.

Doug fumbled to form a response.

Candace nodded. "There's a backlash because change is difficult. There is backlash because it is easier to blame someone that differs from you for your hardship than to actively look for solutions. That's why. Change always feels like it happened overnight. It doesn't."

"What does that have to do with this?" Doug asked.

"Everything. We can implement policy. That doesn't mean the policy will work. I'm not prepared to bite off more than we can chew. Immigration is too important. It directly impacts people's lives in more ways than you are considering. We have to act thoughtfully and holistically, Doug."

"It is one of the things people expect from you," he offered.

"Everyone expects something from me." Candace chuckled. "And, everyone will be disappointed at some point. We're not walking into this thinking about another election. That's not why I ran this campaign."

"I understand, but your approval ratings will impact the effectiveness of Congress."

"Yes, they will," Candace agreed. "Slow and steady. Let's bank a win on infrastructure and tax reform. Let's get some needed reform on student debt first."

"Popular, but," Doug began.

"It's not about popularity. It brings people to the table. Let them hash it out, argue, spit, complain, and ultimately let's get it done. It creates relationships,

Doug. Whether you think so or not, that's how change happens in life. And, politics is just like life. It's all about people and personality. You have to learn how to bring people together. That's where we'll start. That doesn't mean we won't be laying the groundwork behind the scenes. We have a narrow majority in the Senate and a narrow minority in the House. 'A house divided against itself cannot stand.' Our scenario wasn't Lincoln's. His words apply. We cannot tackle this issue as Democrats and Republicans first. We have to address it as citizens." Candace looked at Dana. "Now, where are we at with Deirdre McDermott? Have we reached out about Agriculture?"

Grant nodded. "I have a call scheduled for you at three."

"Good. Next?"

"JD?"

"Yeah?"

Michelle laughed. "Where were you?"

"I'm sorry."

"It's okay. Are you okay?"

Jameson sighed lightly. "Yeah."

Michelle smirked.

"I am," Jameson said. "I'm not good at this, Shell."

"What 'this' are we talking about?"

"Figuring out what's best to get involved with."

Michelle nodded. Jameson was setting her agenda — what areas would she focus on as the president's wife? "What are you struggling with?" Michelle asked.

"Everything?"

"JD, stop trying so hard."

"There are a million things that need attention."

"What do you feel passionate about?"

"All of them?" Jameson groaned.

Michelle laughed. "And, you think you and Mom aren't alike?"

"What do you mean?"

"This is what she goes through every day, JD. Everything requires her attention at some point. The question she has to answer now is what demands her attention where she can have the most dramatic effect. What do you want to pour your energy into?"

"Aside from working with LGBTQ youth; I probably should say community policing."

"Not unless that is what your heart and head are telling you."

Jameson sighed again.

"What is your heart telling you?"

"Adoption," Jameson said. "There are so many kids like Cooper who never find a home, Shell. They get lost in the system. There has to be a way to improve the system and to encourage people to consider fostering or adopting older kids like Coop."

Michelle smiled.

"Bad idea?" Jameson asked.

"I think it's a wonderful idea, JD."

"Really?"

"Yes, really. Why don't you think so?"

"I don't know, Shell. Everyone knows about my family. It feels like I should be focused on combatting addiction or bridging communities and law enforcement."

"Cooper is your family."

"You know what I mean."

"I do, but I don't think you're seeing the bigger picture."

"Which is?" Jameson asked.

"JD, lots of the kids who fall through the system you are talking about end up confronting addiction, at odds with law enforcement. Dealing with kids like Coop who don't get the same chance, helping them find that chance for a family, that will make a difference in more ways than you are thinking about."

"But is that enough?"

"What's enough?" Michelle replied. "And, JD? You don't have to choose one thing. Concentrate on improving life for kids like Coop, on bringing awareness to adoption. Make that year one's focus. See where it leads. You can still lend your name and your time to the other things you care about. Stop second-guessing yourself."

"Thanks, Shell."

"It's what I do."

Jameson laughed. "What about my staff?"

"I've been looking at that."

"And?"

"I think you should talk to Mom about bringing Laura onto your team."

"Laura? Your mom was hoping Laura could help her."

"I think what Mom is hoping is that Laura can find her feet again, find her confidence to be who she is despite her father — publicly."

"But she has…"

"Your office and Mom's will have to coordinate, JD."

Jameson cringed. It sounded official, clinical — cold. Her office would have to coordinate with Candace's? "I'm not a contractor, Shell."

"You kind of are, JD."

Jameson groaned.

"Mom won't put it that way; I will. Your agenda reflects on her administration. You two aren't going to be hashing out schedules over Chinese Take-out."

"Better not tell your mother that."

Michelle laughed. "You know what I mean."

"I do, but I don't have to like it."

"No, you don't. It's not as awful as it sounds."

"I don't know; it sounds pretty awful."

"That's one reason I think Laura would be great. She's got a pulse on all these things."

"What would she do?"

"Here's the beauty of your job as First Lesbo."

"Classy, Shell."

Michelle grinned. "I've been wanting to say that since Mom won," she confessed.

"It's a title of distinction," Jameson replied with a roll of her eyes.

"Actually, it is," Michelle said. "It's a big deal, JD."

"I know."

"Here's the fun part; you get to create your office. You can make up a title."

"Seriously?"

"Yep."

"Huh. What were you thinking?"

"Liaison to Oval Office Operations."

"Sounds formal."

Michelle laughed. "It would be. Laura would work directly with you and your staff and coordinate your efforts with Mom's Personal Secretary and Aide. It would mean she'd interact with you both."

"Can I do that? Hire my daughter-in-law?"

"She's not shaping policy. Frankly, I think it's a better idea for Mom too. It will accomplish what Mom is hoping, give you someone you trust close, and keep tongues from wagging about nepotism."

"Do you think Laura would want to work with me?"

"Would you want her to? I think that's the important question to answer first."

Jameson smiled. She would love to work with Laura. Laura was closer to Candace than to Jameson. It would give her a chance to build a rapport with Jonah's wife, one without Jonah or Candace's direct influence. "I think I would."

"Good. So, let's look at who else you will need."

⁓⁂⁓

Cassidy watched Candace thoughtfully as they sipped their glasses of wine. It was unusual for Candace to appear tense. Tonight, stress seemed to pour off the future president. "Do you want to talk about it?" Cassidy asked.

"Yes and no," Candace said.

"I can understand that."

"It must've been hard dropping Dylan back at school." Candace sought to keep the conversation on Cassidy's life.

Cassidy sipped her wine. "It just about killed me. I think it was worse for Alex."

"I remember when Marianne left. I thought it would get easier with Shell and Jonah."

"Did it?"

"Nope."

Cassidy laughed. "Fabulous."

"You have plenty of time, Cassidy."

"It goes by so fast," Cassidy said. "I'll tell you the truth; some days I am exhausted. Between Mackenzie's activities, the twins, and Fallon, sometimes I forget to breathe."

Candace nodded.

"What's bothering you?" Cassidy wondered. "It's not work."

Candace sighed. "Jameson told me she doesn't think that we should have any more children."

"Not what you wanted to hear?"

"Honestly?"

"Honestly."

"I thought it was."

Cassidy smiled. She was hardly surprised by Candace's reaction. "You know, when I told Alex I wanted to try one more time, she balked."

"Really?"

"Really. Then, when I miscarried, I thought that was it. Reluctant doesn't begin to describe Alex's feelings when I still wanted to keep trying."

"Loss is never easy," Candace offered.

"No, it isn't."

Lately, Candace's thoughts had been wandering back to the baby she'd lost more than was usual. "I've been thinking about Lucas a lot lately. I'm not sure why."

"Change tends to do that," Cassidy observed. "It does for me. I think it's the uncertainty. When my father... Well, when he reappeared in my life, I found myself thinking about all the losses—my grandparents, Chris, Alex's father—all of it. It took me a while to process everything."

Candace understood perfectly. Change had a way of making a person examine the paths they'd chosen in life, and the paths that had been chosen for them. "I'm not sure why it has me rattled."

"Because you love JD, and family is important to you."

Candace sighed. That was true. It was more than that, and Candace didn't want to admit all the things that were driving her feelings. She hated having no control over her life. She suddenly felt old. She felt time pressing in on her life. That bothered her.

"Candace?"

"It just slips by so fast, Cassidy. I hope Jameson realizes that."

"It does. Are you worried that she'll change her mind and it will be too late?"

"That's part of it. If I were twenty years younger, she'd have wanted that for us."

"You don't know that," Cassidy said.

"I do."

"Candace," Cassidy began gently. "Are you feeling guilty?"

"Maybe I am."

"You know that JD wouldn't want you to feel that way."

"I know, but sometimes I can't help it. I don't want her to look back one day and wish she'd made different decisions."

"I think we all do that," Cassidy offered.

"I suppose we do."

"I always tell Dylan that it's normal to wonder. What's not healthy is dwelling on the past. I can't tell you how many times I've battled with myself over Chris. Why did I marry him? Why did I stay all those years?" Cassidy shook her head. "The only answer I can come up with is that if I hadn't, I wouldn't have the life I do now. I know that. It doesn't mean I never think about it."

Candace smiled genuinely. Cassidy's words reminded her why Cassidy had become her best friend. Candace had given similar advice to all three of her children. Sometimes, what you knew and what you felt were at odds. "Thanks."

"For what?"

"For being here this weekend," Candace said.

Cassidy was happy to spend a weekend with Candace. Much of their time would be spent working. It didn't matter; work always led to personal discussions for the pair. "I think I should be thanking you."

"Hardly."

"No, I mean it." Cassidy sipped her wine and set it aside. "I love Alex. God knows, I love our parents and our kids, but…"

"But sometimes you need someone to talk to who is removed from it all," Candace said.

"Exactly," Cassidy agreed. "You never know, JD might change her mind." Cassidy chuckled at Candace's doubtful expression. "Can I offer you a piece of advice?"

"Please."

"If it's something you want, you should tell JD."

Candace wasn't sure that she did want to have any more children. She'd put those longings to bed long before she'd married Jameson. It was odd to her; she had thought that adopting Cooper would quell any stirrings she or Jameson might experience. Cooper's presence in their lives seemed to have accomplished the opposite. Candace questioned what nagged at her more; the idea that she and Jameson would never have a baby together, or the notion that the decision was out of her hands. "I'm not sure what I want. There is so much going on in our lives right now — this is the last thing I should be thinking about."

Cassidy laughed. "That's usually how it happens."

Candace finally joined in Cassidy's laughter. "True."

"Give it a little time," Cassidy advised. "You just said it; your cup runneth over — and not all in the best of ways. Most people have a thousand moving pieces to deal with. You have a billion. Get through the next few months. I'll bet things will seem clearer then."

"I hope so."

Cassidy decided to shift gears. "How goes everything else?"

"Other than the fact that I nearly killed Doug today? Not bad."

"Oh, no."

"You would think I'd be used to it by now."

"What's that?" Cassidy asked.

"Dealing with advisers and legislators is like dealing with my kids—not my grandkids or Cooper—The Three Stooges. Something happens when they hit puberty. They suddenly go deaf. Then, after they pass it; they develop selective hearing. I swear."

Cassidy nearly spit out her wine. "Are you trying to kill me?" She laughed.

"It's the truth."

"I wonder if that's what our parents think about us."

"Guaranteed," Candace said. "Tell me again why I wanted this job?"

"Because you can do it better than anyone else who was willing to try."

Candace massaged her eyes. Could she? She had to.

"You can," Cassidy said. "You will. What happened with Doug?"

"He means well. They all mean well." Candace chuckled. "He thinks we can solve the world's problems in one legislative session." She rolled her eyes. "They all do."

"They're excited."

"Understatement."

Cassidy suddenly understood what had Candace in knots. Everyone around Candace was brimming with enthusiasm and excitement. They saw possibility everywhere. Someone had to temper their eagerness. That someone was Candace. On the public stage, Candace delivered optimistic, sometimes lofty speeches. Cassidy had learned that Candace never imparted sentiment she didn't believe. When the lights dimmed, and the stage cleared, Candace became the voice of reason. "In other words, you get to play Mom all day."

Candace laughed. She often felt as though she were playing everyone's mother. "It's not that I don't appreciate their passion," she told Cassidy. "I do. Passion without temperance can run the best policy off the tracks before it gets started. I know it will get better when I am in the role and have a cabinet in place. Right now, everything is in limbo."

"I know it is," Cassidy said.

Nothing in Candace's life felt steady except Jameson. She was living between worlds. Everyone was forced to live in the present no matter how they might prefer the past or the future. Candace's present lacked foundation. She had a temporary home, a temporary staff, her past seemed determined to niggle at her thoughts, and the future seemed to plague her emotions.

"It's easy to feel out of balance when nothing is settled," Cassidy said.

"It is."

"I know it probably feels like an eternity; it's only ten more days."

Candace's heart sped up. "Is that all?"

"Something tells me we need more wine."

Candace winked. "What do you think?"

"About?" Cassidy asked.

"Do you think I'll be the first president to write an Inauguration speech hung over?"

Cassidy and Candace fell into a fit of laughter. Candace squeezed her friend's hand. Cassidy's company seemed the perfect prescription for what had been ailing her. Friendship was a balm for the soul.

❦

"Are they getting drunk in there?" Michelle asked Jameson.

Jameson smiled. The sound of Candace's laughter lifted her spirits. "I hope they are," she said.

"Why? Hoping she'll need to repent later?" Michelle poked.

"That would be a bonus."

"Gross, JD."

"Just because we own a Bible, doesn't mean we're nuns."

Michelle rolled her eyes. "You made my mother a nymphomaniac."

Jameson burst into laughter. *If only.*

CHAPTER EIGHT

JANUARY 21ST

Jameson looked out the window of the SUV as it rolled through the streets of Washington DC. If it seemed surreal now, she could hardly imagine how she would react the next day. She'd needed to get away from the chaos at home. Tomorrow, Candace would become the forty-fifth president. Jameson would stand beside her wife as Candace laid her hand on the Bible that her close friend John Merrow had sworn his oath upon.

Barricades already denied access to certain streets. Grandstands had been erected along the parade route. Jameson shook her head. *Unreal.*

"Don?" Jameson called up to the Secret Service agent in charge of her detail.

"Yes, Ms. Reid?"

"Can we head over to the Capitol?"

"You want to go there now?"

"Yeah. Is that a problem?"

"I'd like to make a few calls."

Jameson sighed with frustration. It wasn't unusual for there to be threats on Candace. She hated that reality. She'd been dealing with the knowledge of threats since Candace announced her candidacy. There had been a few issues when Candace was governor, nothing close to what Candace faced as a presidential candidate. Jameson was positive that would seem like child's play after tomorrow. She closed her eyes and rubbed her temples. A myriad of emotions ran through her: excitement, anxiety, pride, love, disbelief — hopefulness. She'd thought she was prepared for Candace's new role. She was prepared to be supportive. She was prepared to walk any path she needed to as Candace's wife. Jameson doubted that anyone was ready for their wife to become The President of the United States. She wondered if she would ever fully grasp that this was real. She was about to become First Lady. That thought made her laugh.

"Are you all right?" Agent Don Reardon asked.

"Just wondering if I am in some strange version of *The Truman Show.*"

Reardon chuckled. He looked at the driver next to him. "You heard the boss, the Capitol it is."

Jameson closed her eyes again. She needed to see it all unfolding if she had any hope of believing tomorrow was real. She'd left Candace to rehearse her speech with Michelle. Most of the family had already arrived in DC. Candace's brothers were due to arrive later that afternoon. Jonah, Laura, Melanie and Michelle and their children were staying at the townhouse. Pearl, Jameson's parents, Marianne, Scott, Maddie and Spencer would make the move to Blair House

with Candace and Jameson. Jameson had been surprised when Candace had suggested it. They both
needed a degree of stability. It made sense. She hoped
that the presence of family might ease her nervousness.

Jameson's eyes roamed over the approaching
scene. She took a deep breath. The flags draped over
the Capitol were impressive even at a distance. She
smiled at a stand selling merchandise adorned with
Candace's face. "Can you pull over?"

"Here?" Agent Reardon asked.

"Yes."

Reardon instructed the driver to comply. He ex-
ited the car and opened Jameson's door. The agent
forced himself not to laugh at Jameson's childlike expression. He accompanied her a few paces to the small
cart that was decorated with T-shirts, buttons, hats, and
Mardi Gras style beads in red, white, and blue.

"Hi," Jameson strolled up to the vendor.

The young man's jaw dropped.

"I was wondering how much your T-shirts are."

The vendor tried to speak but nothing seemed to
pass his lips.

Jameson chuckled. She extended her hand. "I'm
JD."

"You're the president's wife."

"Not yet. I mean, yes, Candace is my wife. She's
not the president *yet*."

"Wow. I…"

"How much for the T-shirts?" Jameson asked again.

"Take one," he said.

Jameson smiled. "I can't do that. How much?"

"They're fifteen bucks."

"Cash only?"

He nodded. Jameson reached into her jacket pocket and pulled out her wallet. It was unusual for her to carry any cash. She'd gotten some cash the day before to give to Marianne and Scott. They were staying in DC for the rest of the week and planned to take the kids on a sightseeing jaunt after the Inaugural festivities. She pulled out three fifty-dollar bills. "If my math is right, that covers ten shirts."

The young man nodded. "Which ones?"

Jameson pointed to an artistic representation of Candace smiling with the Inauguration date emblazoned beneath her likeness. "How about that one? Wait, do you have any for kids?"

"Not really."

Jameson pondered the thought. "How much are the buttons?"

"Five, but..."

"Hold on," Jameson said. She dug in her wallet again. "Here." She handed him a twenty. "I'll take four buttons too. The kids will like those better anyway."

The man nodded. He filled a bag with Jameson's items and looked at her. He picked up a small bag of tiny pins. "Take them," he said.

"I can't take them without paying you."

He shrugged. "I wish you would. I can make more tonight."

"You made them?"

"Yeah; and designed them."

"Seriously?" Jameson asked.

He nodded.

"What's your name?"

"Rick."

Jameson smiled. "Our son-in-law's name was Rick."

"Yeah, I know."

"So, is this a good gig?"

"If you can get the permit; yeah. It helps pay my tuition."

"You're a student?"

"Yeah."

Jameson continued the conversation curiously. "What are you studying?"

"Law at Georgetown."

"I'm impressed."

"Hey, you're the one married to the president."

"Not yet," Jameson winked. "Don't ask me how that happened." She laughed. "I got lucky."

"Thanks," he said.

"For what?" Jameson wondered.

"For buying and for talking."

"A lawyer who designs shirts and buttons. There's a story there," Jameson said.

"I used to want to be an artist."

"Used to?"

"Yeah. It's a long story."

Jameson nodded. She was intrigued by the young man. "Are you going to be out here tomorrow?"

"I hope so," he said. "Sometimes they make us move when there's a big event."

"I'll bet."

"I voted for her," he said.

Jameson grinned. "Me too."

He laughed. "I hope she likes the shirt."

"She will. Hey, you designed this; right? I mean, the picture. I've never seen it before."

"I painted it. Turned it into a graphic print."

"Do you have the original?"

"Yeah?"

"How much do you want for it?"

"For my painting?"

"Yeah."

"Are you serious?"

"Completely. I've been wondering what I could get Candace to mark the occasion. This would be perfect."

"Do you think she'd want it?"

"She'll love it. And the fact that a young man named Rick who's studying law and voted for her painted it? Bonus points. So, how much?"

"I don't know, Two hundred maybe?"

Jameson nodded. She looked at Agent Reardon. "Do you have anything to write with?"

Rick grabbed a notebook and pen. "Here."

Jameson pushed it back. "Write down where I can send you a check."

He scribbled down an address.

"This is where you live?" Jameson inquired.

"Yeah."

"So, would it be okay if I sent someone over with the check tonight to pick up the painting?"

"Sure."

"Are you sure? I don't want to inconvenience you."

"Are you kidding? I'll be home by five."

Jameson smiled at his enthusiasm. "Perfect. Thanks, Rick. You know, our son Jonah is a pretty talented artist too."

"Really?"

"He doesn't think so. He is; so is our son Cooper. Well, if what you like in art is trains and dinosaurs or genies."

Rick laughed. "Thanks again, Ms. Reid."

"JD," Jameson said. She held out her hand again and shook his. "Just JD. And, thank you." She started to walk away and turned back. "I'd love to hear that story sometime," she told him.

He watched as Jameson climbed back into the car. "What just happened?" he muttered.

"Are you nervous?" Maureen asked Candace.

"A little. I don't think it's hit me yet."

"I can't even imagine. I know it hasn't hit me. My daughter-in-law is actually going to be the president tomorrow."

"Somehow, hearing you say it makes it seem real."

"How's JD holding up?"

"You know Jameson; she's been the picture of calm on the outside this week," Candace said.

"But?"

"She's nervous. I can tell. She's also excited."

"She's proud of you. We all are."

"I have a lot to do to earn that," Candace said. "The election was the easy part."

"Says you."

"It's the truth," Candace offered.

"And you? Are you excited?"

"I don't know if that's the word I'd use. More like awestruck."

Maureen smiled. "I still can't imagine."

"Jameson keeps telling me to enjoy tomorrow."

"She's right."

"I know. The truth is that there will be a million things waiting on my desk the moment we step through the White House doors."

"Regrets?" Maureen wondered.

"I wish I could say yes, but no; I don't regret any of it. I do understand that it's not about elections any longer. The speeches do matter. Tomorrow matters. It sets the tone for my administration."

Maureen had heard Candace practicing her speech with Michelle. She thought it combined both lofty idealism and practical principle — the foundations of Candace's campaign. She admired that about Candace. Candace could schmooze with the best of hobnob society. She exuded confidence and eloquence in her public demeanor, but she never appeared aloof or snobbish. And, Candace did not lie. Maureen knew as well as anyone that Candace couldn't always offer details about her plans, but she always endeavored to be upfront about the spirit of her intentions and her beliefs. Maureen respected her daughter-in-law as a woman and as a policy-maker.

"From what I heard, you have nothing to worry about." Maureen offered.

"Mmm. It's difficult to address our issues and remain idealistic at times. It can make a person sound arrogant or it can instill a sense of optimism. It's always a gamble," Candace said. "Hopefully, it will speak to more people than those who carried me through the election, at least, to some of them."

Candace grew quiet. Maureen was curious where Candace's thoughts had traveled.

"I know it will take time," Candace said. "For people to move past their prejudices, whatever they may be—that I'm a Democrat or that I'm a woman or that I'm a lesbian. Some never will. I know that. I can't accept that. If I do, I'm in danger of falling into the trap called complacency. I haven't taken the oath, and I see evidence of that malady everywhere."

"Complacency?"

"Yes. Don't get me wrong; I know the American people by and large believe that this town is self-absorbed. I wish I could say they're wrong."

Maureen listened intently. She loved to discuss politics with Candace. As a history teacher, Jameson's mother had always been fascinated by government. Political science classes and history books offered comparatively little insight when held up to a conversation with Candace. Candace had spent a lifetime around politics, and most of her adulthood holding office. She had a command of more than facts and figures, laws and traditions. Candace had developed an acute understanding of the way relationships motivated change. She also provided a unique perspective on government's role in shaping public perception. It seemed to Maureen that Candace had been mulling over her many years of experience as she prepared to take office. She wondered if this transitional period had offered the next president any new revelations.

Candace continued to share her thoughts. "I know people see us as removed from them. The truth is, we are. Most of us have been running campaigns and sitting in conference meetings, attending roll calls longer than many of our constituents have been voting." She chuckled. "It's not a lack of care that drives the stagnation in Washington. It is, I'm afraid, a lack of connection to the people who sent us here. It's complacency. Too much comfort with what is familiar and not enough courage to pursue something new. We've lost our imagination, Maureen. Perhaps with it, we've also lost our resolve."

"Candace, I don't mean to speak out of turn. I've watched you with people. Connecting to others is not a problem for you."

"No. But it would be easy for it to become mechanical. That doesn't happen because people don't care. There are so many moving parts. There is always the next campaign. There are competing agendas. It's easy to get lost in all of it."

"Are you worried that people won't come to the table?" Maureen asked.

"Not worried—aware. The legislature needs to connect to my vision or they need to connect with me. If they don't, I need to find a way to get their constituents to make that leap. That will force their hand. It's not unlike campaigning. It is more nuanced, and the stakes are much higher. The battle has already begun. My agenda begins the moment I step onto that platform tomorrow. I know that."

Maureen regarded Candace thoughtfully. She sat in awe of Jameson's wife. Candace was articulate and intelligent. Many people possessed those qualities. It was Candace's earnest desire to make a difference that set her apart in Maureen's eyes. Candace continued to connect people with issues and with her because she demanded she never forget that why she held office. She lacked hubris. "You know," Maureen began. "I think there is one thing you left out."

"What's that?"

"I don't have the seat you do," Maureen offered. "I'm not meeting with Congressional leaders or heads of state. I'm not conversing with the president in the Oval Office. I sit at the kitchen table and watch from afar like the most people. I have an advantage over them. I get to sit across from you at my kitchen table from time to time. I know you, Candace. There is more than chaos at work, more than complacency. There's also ego."

Candace smiled. Managing people's egos was half the battle in a room full of politicians.

"I don't think anyone can get where you are without possessing confidence. The difference between confidence and hubris is measurable. I've never heard you speak with self-importance. You always talk about your role, not your rein."

Candace chuckled. "We do have some self-appointed kings and queens in our midst."

"I can't imagine what you are feeling now. I can't. I've tried. It has to be overwhelming. If anyone can make a difference, it's you."

Candace took Maureen's hand. "Thank you."

"After managing this family, and my daughter; the world should be a cinch."

"Maybe I can entice the world with my lasagna like I do this family."

"Or you could offer them wine."

Candace burst out laughing. "I might just add that to the top of my agenda."

꧁꧂

Rick Blunt opened the door to his apartment and felt his jaw drop for the second time that day.

"You must be Rick," Michelle said.

"Yeah."

Michelle chuckled at the realization the young man had recognized her immediately. "I still get to wander freely," she said. "For the most part." She gestured to the agent standing a few paces behind her. "Shell," she introduced herself.

"Hi. I'm sorry. It's not every day you meet the president's family."

"Well, we're not quite the president's family yet."

"You sound like Ms. Reid."

"JD's pretty smart. Don't ever tell her I admitted that."

He chuckled. "Come in. I was just about to wrap the canvas."

Michelle took a step inside. The painting immediately caught her attention. "Wow. That's it?"

He nodded.

"It's incredible."

"Really?"

"Yeah. JD said you were studying law. Why? You're like Picasso or something."

"Hardly," he replied. "It's a long story."

"Yeah, she mentioned that too." Michelle watched as the young man wrapped the canvas in plastic and placed it in a cardboard shell. "My mom is going to flip when she sees that."

"Really?"

Michelle laughed. "You like that word, huh?"

"Sorry, I guess I'm a little nervous."

"Don't be."

"Easy for you to say."

"Nah. I'm a teacher by trade," Michelle offered. "And a mom. That's me."

"And, Candace Reid's daughter."

"There is that." Michelle grinned. "She's just Mom to me," Michelle said.

"Yeah, not to most of us."

Michelle nodded. No matter how much time she spent on the campaign trail with her mother, she was never able to fully grasp the way people perceived Candace. "So, why law?"

He sighed. "It's not that interesting."

"I doubt that."

Rick hesitated.

"Hey, don't worry about it. I'm just curious. I like lawyers. My mom and dad both were lawyers."

"My father went to prison when I turned twenty," Rick explained.

"And that made you want to learn law?"

"He didn't have the money for an attorney."

Michelle sighed. "I'm sorry."

"It happens. It happens to addicts all the time," he replied.

"I don't mean to pry; was it a drug conviction?"

He nodded. "Third offense. They hit him with intent to sell. He'll be in prison for another ten years."

"I'm sorry."

"Art is great. I couldn't do anything to help him as an artist. Painting was never going to help him." He taped the box around the painting of Candace. "It's all set."

Michelle reached into her coat pocket and pulled out an envelope. "Here."

"Thanks."

"Don't you want to open it?"

"I trust it's good," he joked. He handed Michelle the box.

"Thanks," she said.

He walked Michelle to the door and opened it. "Umm," he fumbled. "Tell your mother I'm glad she's the one up there tomorrow."

Michelle gestured to the envelope in his hand. "Tell her yourself," she said with a wink.

He watched Michelle disappear with her escort down the hallway and opened the envelope. He unfolded a piece of paper and gasped at the tickets inside. Then his eyes fell to the writing.

Rick,

I enjoyed meeting you this afternoon. Your work is amazing. I know Candace is going to cherish it. I also know my wife; she'll want to thank you herself. I hope you aren't too busy tomorrow evening and can find someone to accompany you. I'd like you to be our guest at the Arts and Culture Ball. I'm sure it'll be more colorful than some of the other functions we have to attend.

I hope Shell didn't give away all our family secrets. I look forward to seeing you tomorrow. Maybe you'd be willing to tell us your story. I'd love to hear it.

Hope to see you tomorrow night. Thanks again.
JD

Rick fished in the envelope for the folded check. "Oh, my god," he held his breath. His eyes scanned the comment line.

It's worth a lot more than two-hundred bucks.

He shook his head. "Five-thousand dollars? Is she insane?" He laughed. "At least, I can afford a tux for the ball."

🦋🦋

"Where did you disappear to?" Candace asked when Jameson walked into the bedroom they were sharing.

"I didn't disappear."

"You most certainly did."

"Close your eyes."

"Are you going to disappear again?"

"I'm not Houdini. Just close your eyes."

Candace complied reluctantly.

Jameson grabbed her gift for Candace from the hallway. She'd asked Michelle to wrap it for her. Shell may have delighted in giving Jameson a hard time; it seemed she understood that this gift was special. Jameson was amazed at the beautiful paper that covered the canvas. She was anxious to give it to Candace. She walked toward the bed where Candace was seated and placed the package on the floor at her feet. "Okay, open your eyes."

Candace's eyes narrowed at the colorful package. "What's this?"

"Open it," Jameson suggested.

"Jameson, you didn't need to get me anything."

Jameson made no reply. She was intent on watching Candace's expression as she unwrapped the picture.

Candace tore away the paper carefully. "Jameson... Where did you ... When did you..."

"Do you like it?"

"It's... It's gorgeous."

"Like you."

Candace smiled through watery eyes.

"When I was out today, we passed a street vendor." Jameson reached behind a chair and retrieved the items she'd bought earlier that day. She pulled out a T-shirt. "I saw this and I had to stop."

"You bought a T-shirt?"

"No, I bought ten—one for each of us. And, some buttons for the kids."

Candace shook her head affectionately.

"Anyway, I started talking to the kid who was selling them. He told me he painted the picture and turned it into merchandise."

"Industrious."

"I thought so too." Jameson took a breath. "He was so nervous," she chuckled. "He reminded me a bit of Cooper the first time I met him, only older."

Candace grinned.

"I asked him if he had the original, and he did, so…"

"I love it."

"I wanted you to have something special. It's part of the reason I went out. I never expected to end up finding what I wanted from a kid selling T-shirts."

"Something tells me there is more to this story."

Jameson nodded. "I talked to him for a while. He's a law student at Georgetown."

"Law?" Candace looked at the painting.

"I know; I had the same reaction. He said he wanted to be an artist once. Now, he sells the stuff to help pay his tuition for law school."

"You liked him."

"I did. His name is Rick."

Candace took a deep breath and nodded.

"Is it strange?"

"What's that?" Candace asked.

"I feel like it was a sign—me asking Don to drive by The Capitol—finding that stand, meeting him."

"I don't think it's strange at all."

"I had Shell pick up the painting while we were at dinner."

Candace waited, knowing there was more to Jameson's story.

"I invited him to the Arts and Culture Ball."

Candace smiled brightly.

"Is that okay?"

Candace set the painting aside and made her way to Jameson. "It's more than okay."

Jameson sighed with relief.

"I love you." Candace brought her lips to Jameson's. "So much, Jameson."

"So, you like the painting?"

"I love it. I love all the reasons you bought it. I love that you thought to invite that young man. You," Candace took Jameson's face in her hands. "Remind me every day why I love you so much."

"It's just a painting."

"No, it isn't. It's the reasons you chose that painting. It's the time you took to talk to that young man. It's the thought you had to send Shell to get it while we were at dinner, and the gesture you made by inviting him tomorrow. I couldn't ask for a better partner, Jameson. Not just as my wife, but as a parent, and as a president."

"I think you give me too much credit."

"Not at all," Candace disagreed. Her fingertips caressed Jameson's cheeks. "Let me make love to you."

Jameson lost her breath the moment Candace's lips found hers again. When, she wondered, would that feeling end? Never.

Every ounce of tension and apprehension faded into oblivion the moment Candace felt Jameson's tongue dance with hers. Jameson moaned, and her lips became demanding, seeking more with urgency. Candace pulled back and tugged gently on Jameson's bottom lip with her teeth. "Shh."

Candace's fingertips trailed down the side of Jameson's neck like a whisper, barely felt yet somehow making Jameson aware of every nerve in her body.

"Candace," Jameson sighed through her wife's name.

Candace's body pulsed with desire fueled by raw emotion. The irony of love always astounded her. Jameson was both the wind in the sails of Candace's life and the anchor that kept her steady. Contradiction became complement; it's what made being in love intoxicating. Love never overshadowed the desire that burned in Candace's veins when she touched Jameson. Love didn't taper the power of lust; it ignited the spark between them. Candace had already become lost in the exploration of the woman she loved. She let her lips fall to the hollow of Jameson's throat, her tongue sliding lower until it reached the opening of Jameson's blouse.

Jameson closed her eyes. She could feel Candace's fingers tugging at the buttons of her shirt, methodically releasing them one by one. The warmth of Candace's mouth continued on its downward path and lingered over Jameson's cleavage until Candace released the final button. Jameson sighed when she felt the blouse pushed aside and off her shoulders. Less than a second passed and her bra pooled at her feet beside the discarded blouse. Her heart hammered wildly. She opened her eyes and met Candace's passionate gaze. Could Candace be sexier? Jameson lost her breath at the sight. How had she managed to get this lucky? The woman looking at her was everything; not because Candace had accomplished amazing things or because she was a wonderful mother. It wasn't because Candace was beautiful or intelligent. It wasn't only the compassion that lingered in every touch Candace offered Jameson; it was all of it, every piece that drew Jameson to Candace. She'd often heard people say that it was possible to love more than one person. Jameson felt certain she would never love another human being as deeply or as completely as she loved her wife. She'd discovered love with Candace; love that hungered for closeness.

Candace let her mouth surround Jameson's nipple softly. She closed her eyes and enjoyed the response her tender sucking elicited. Her hands dropped to Jameson's hips. Jameson's breath was coming in short, desperate pants. Candace moved one hand to tease Jameson's other breast. She was rewarded with a gasp of surprise followed by a grateful moan. Tiny shock waves erupted over her skin, like static electricity in the winter. Her nipples tingled with desire and her core began to pound gently with need. She pushed Jameson back until Jameson fell softly onto the bed. Her hands trembled slightly as she pulled Jameson's jeans down. More—she needed more. She needed all of Jameson. The sound of Jameson's voice startled her.

"Candace, please?"

Candace looked up at Jameson. "Please? What do you want, love?"

Jameson's licked her lips. "I need to feel you against me," she confessed. "Just against me, Candace. Please?"

Candace stood. She smiled at Jameson and slowly undressed for her. Jameson's eyes had glossed over. The air crackled with energy. She lowered herself and hovered above Jameson. "I love you," she promised.

Jameson's hands drew Candace closer until no air existed between them, only two warm bodies pressed together, gliding sensually against one another. Her mouth claimed Candace's with a possessive kiss. Closer. She needed to be closer. Jameson groaned when Candace's thigh slid between her legs.

"So perfect," Candace whispered in Jameson's ear. "So perfect against me."

Jameson tasted the flesh behind Candace's ear, nipping and sucking until Candace began to moan constantly. She wanted to turn them in the bed, descend Candace's body like a wolf stalking its prey. Her mind rolled through images of Candace's face contorting with pleasure. She couldn't tear herself away. More than release, she needed Candace near.

Candace pressed her thigh against Jameson's heated center. It nearly sent Jameson over the edge and into oblivion. How could she relinquish her hold? She could almost taste Jameson on her lips. God, she wanted to taste Jameson. The longer they continued to glide

together, the more desperate Candace became. Her
hand traced a line from Jameson's shoulder to her hip
and then tracked inward. "Yes," she hissed.

Jameson held onto Candace. She felt Candace
slide two fingers inside her, softly at first, increasing in
force with each thrust. She struggled to breathe, lost in
the fantasies that unbridled sensation elicited. Her hips
rose without her permission. Her head fell back, and
she heard herself release a strangled cry of pleasure.
Candace had control of her body. Candace commanded
her heart, and she would gladly give it all to the
woman she loved.

The sight of Jameson in the throes of ecstasy
eclipsed the majesty of any sunrise or sunset Candace
had ever witnessed. There was no wonder in the world
that compared to the view Candace had at the moment.
Sublime, arousing, exciting, breathtaking — Jameson's
movements, the sounds escaping the back of her throat,
the feel of Jameson's fingertips pressing into Candace's
flesh — it heralded completion. Candace placed her lips
a breath away from Jameson's. "You are everything,
Jameson — everything to me," she said.

Jameson fell away. Candace's tongue brushed
across her lips, seeking entrance. Jameson granted the
request eagerly. Candace gentled their kiss immediately, tenderly inviting Jameson to search and explore. It
was the softest kiss Jameson had ever experienced, as if
Candace poured every memory they shared, each
dream they dared dream, every word and touch that

had passed between them into one kiss. She felt Candace's thumb circle her center and press against her clit while she thrust deeply with her fingers. Jameson's world exploded into an array of color and light. Her cries were swallowed by Candace's lingering kiss. Her body rose from the bed, meeting Candace's, pleading for more. God, she wanted more. Could there be more?

Candace quivered at the power of Jameson's release. Jameson was pulling her closer in desperation. She understood the silent request and moved to straddle Jameson's hips. She smiled when Jameson opened her eyes.

Jameson sucked in a ragged breath. *Candace.* "God, you are beautiful," Jameson said. Her hands stretched to fondle Candace's breasts as Candace brought them together intimately. The warmth of Candace's arousal against her caused Jameson's eyelids to flutter and close.

"Jameson," Candace called. "Stay with me."

Jameson forced her eyes to open. She sighed. She loved to watch Candace move with her. She licked her lips. Her thumbs brushed over Candace's nipples.

"Jameson…"

Jameson's touch remained tender. She tugged at her bottom lip with her teeth when Candace's fingers covered her nipples. Together, they danced the most sensual dance two people can share. She held Candace's gaze even as Candace's body began to submit to the swell of sensations between them. Jameson pinched Candace's nipples lightly.

"Jameson!" Candace's exploded in violent shudders, sending Jameson's body into blissful quivering.

"Candace," Jameson spoke the name reverently. She pulled Candace close and held her as they both continued to tremble. She breathed Candace in.

"Jameson." Candace struggled to speak. She caressed Jameson's face and kissed her on the forehead. "Nothing in this world could mean more to me than you. Don't ever forget that."

"I won't."

"Thank you."

"Why are you thanking me?" Jameson asked.

"For loving me; for letting me love you."

Jameson smiled. "I will always love you."

"You have no idea how much I needed this."

"Yes, I do," Jameson said. "I needed to be close to you too."

Candace slipped into Jameson's arms. "Tomorrow will change everything."

"No. It won't change this," Jameson said. "It won't change how much I love you. No matter what you do, Candace, or where you go; no matter how many things people throw at us, there isn't anything that will ever change how much I love you. That is one thing I can promise you."

Candace shifted to look at Jameson. She smiled lovingly. "Are you still hoping to get acquainted with all the fireplaces in the White House?"

Jameson laughed. "More now than ever."

Candace closed her eyes and let Jameson hold her. For the first time in weeks, reality seemed to set in. Tomorrow, she would become the President of the United States. Many things would change. Jameson would remain both the wind and the anchor in her life. She took a deep breath and savored it.

"See you in the morning, Madame President," Jameson whispered.

Candace held onto Jameson a little tighter. "Yes, you will." She was ready.

CHAPTER NINE

INAUGURATION DAY

The scent of Candace's perfume hovered in the air. Jameson stepped out of the shower and inhaled deeply. Her body still tingled from their lovemaking the night before. She'd experienced nervousness, awe, even fear in the last week as this day approached. This morning, the only emotion that coursed through Jameson was love. She found herself anxiously awaiting the moment she would stand beside Candace as Candace took the Oath of Office. She couldn't wait to listen as Candace stood before the world and delivered her speech. And, if there was anything Jameson looked forward to, it was holding Candace's hand and taking her to the dance floor that evening. Last night had settled the rumblings of doubt that had been churning in her soul. Things would change; not what mattered most.

"Good morning."

Jameson turned to the sound of Candace's voice and was met with an appreciative stare. She smiled when Candace moved toward her seductively. "Aren't we supposed to be heading to a prayer breakfast?"

Candace shrugged. "Well, Shell always says we're excellent students of the Bible."

Jameson accepted a sweet kiss from Candace and laughed. "How are you doing?"

"Surprisingly well," Candace said.

"Nervous?"

"A little," Candace confessed. "Excited."

"Good. You should be."

"What about you?" Candace asked.

"Me? I get to say I'm married to the president in a few hours. Who gets to do that?"

Candace grinned. "You also get to be called The First Lady."

"Hey, if they want to call me a lady, that's their problem."

Candace laughed. "Lunatic." She placed another kiss on Jameson's lips. "I'll see you downstairs?"

"I'll be there in a few minutes."

Candace winked and left the bathroom.

"The First Lady," Jameson mumbled. "I wonder how many of those had my tool belt?"

❦

"How's Mom?" Michelle asked Marianne.

Marianne glanced behind her as she held her phone. "Okay, I think. She seems calm."

"I'd shit my pants if I were her."

"Classy, Shell."

"How about JD?"

"She seems happy this morning."

"They probably don't need to go to church this morning then."

"Good Lord, Shell. Just because JD's in a good mood doesn't mean they were having sex last night."

"Uh-huh."

"Well, good for them if they did. It relaxes me."

"Marianne! Gross!"

"Because you are Mother Teresa."

"Maybe I am."

"Right." Marianne shifted gears. "How is everyone there?"

"Everyone is *there*," Michelle replied. "It's just me and Mel, and Jonah and Laura, and the kids."

"So? How is everyone?"

"Brody can't stop pooping. Hope that passes before we get in the car. Guess he's doing the shitting for all of us."

Marianne laughed. Michelle was nervous. "I should go. I need to get Maddie ready."

"What about Spencer?"

"Mom took Spencer and Cooper upstairs to get them ready a few minutes ago."

"Why is Mom doing that?"

"Because she wanted to," Marianne said. "I think she's trying to keep things as normal as possible for as long as possible."

"For the boys?"

"Oh, I think it's for more than the boys," Marianne replied. "I'll see you in an hour." She smiled at her mother when Candace strolled back into the room.

"Marianne?"

"Yeah?"

"Tell Mom I…"

Marianne smiled. "She's right here. Tell her yourself." She handed Candace her phone. "One guess."

Candace smiled. "Good morning, Shell."

"Hi, Mom."

"How is everything there?"

"Poopy; if you want to know the truth."

Candace chuckled. "I'm not sure I want the details."

"Brody's butt has its own personality this morning."

"I see." Candace looked at Marianne and shook her head.

"She's nervous," Marianne whispered.

"How are you?" Michelle asked her mother.

"Staying away from coffee," Candace said.

"Nervous?"

"Less than I expected. You?"

"Me? I'm good, Mom."

"How about everyone else?"

"They're all in the kitchen having coffee. Well, except Mel. She's having juice."

Candace forced herself not to laugh. "You should go join them. I'll see you at the church in a bit."

"Mom?"

"Hum?"

"I love you."

"I love you too, Shell. I'll see you in a bit." Candace handed the phone back to Marianne.

"In case you wondered; I love you too," Marianne said.

Candace hugged her daughter. "I love you, Marianne."

"I'm so proud of you," Marianne said. She struggled not to become emotional.

Candace pulled back from their embrace and wiped a few falling tears from her daughter's cheek. "I'll miss you too, sweetheart."

Marianne nodded. She sniffled and tried to steady herself. "I'm sorry. I'm so proud to be your daughter."

"Not nearly as proud as I am to be your mother," Candace said. She kissed Marianne's forehead and took her hand. "Come on, let's get Maddie ready."

"You don't have to…"

Candace smiled. "Let's go."

"Nana!" Spencer came barreling into the room.

"Yes?"

"Maddie got gum in her hair!"

Candace laughed. "Let's hope we can find some scissors," she told Marianne. *It never changes.*

❧❧❧

"Are you certain?" President Wallace asked.

"As sure as we can be."

Wallace took a deep breath and let it out slowly. "Where?"

"We can't say that yet."

"Timing?"

"Soon," Secretary of Defense Bryce replied.

"Shit."

"Mr. President, what would you like us to do?"

"Keep everyone on it."

"We have the means to hit one of the strongholds now if you give the order."

Wallace grimaced. "No. That's not my decision to make."

"With due respect, Sir, it is."

"No," Wallace disagreed. "In about three hours there will be a new person sitting here."

"Three hours is an eternity in these situations," Bryce reminded the Commander in Chief.

"I'm aware," Wallace replied.

"If you're worried about optics..."

"I'm not concerned with appearances, Jim. If we make the wrong move, we could set up Candace's administration for a world of pain."

"And, if we don't act, the same thing could happen."

Wallace sighed. He took another long breath and shook his head. "Give me a few minutes."

Candace laughed at her granddaughter. Maddie had discovered a pack of gum in Marianne's bag. If the evidence was correct, she'd chewed every piece just long enough to get it all stuck in her hair.

"Why did you put the gum in your hair?" Marianne asked. She scrambled to cut small pieces out without making her daughter's head look like a patchwork quilt.

"It's pwetty."

"Trust me; it's not pretty," Marianne groaned.

Candace snickered.

"Candace?" Jameson stepped into the bathroom.

"Hey, you."

"President Wallace called," Jameson said. "I don't think it can wait."

Candace nodded. "I'll see you downstairs in a few," she told Marianne. She followed Jameson from the room. "What did he say?"

"Only that he needed to speak with you before we left."

"Thank you," Candace said. She stepped into a private room and accepted her phone from Jameson. "I promise; I'll be right there." She waited for Jameson to leave and called the president's private number.

"Candy."

"Mr. President."

Wallace sighed. "I hate making this call."

"What's going on, Don?"

"I received some intelligence this morning."

"I'm listening."

"There seems to be some movement in Belgium."

"What kind of movement?" Candace inquired.

"It would appear there is a plan to hit American targets in the region."

"What region?"

"Europe."

Candace sighed heavily. "Any specifics?"

"Jim seems to think the embassies in Brussels and Minsk are both vulnerable."

"ISIS?"

The president groaned.

"Don?"

"I don't believe so; no. We're meant to think so."

Candace massaged her brow. "What do we know?"

"The best assessment we have is elements within the SVR are directing the efforts."

"Why would the SVR move on our embassies?"

"You've seen the briefings."

Candace leaned against a large, wooden desk. She had reviewed the Intelligence community's assessment of foreign threats. The Russian Foreign Intelligence

Service topped the list. All indications she had seen suggested that the SVR would launch white-collar attacks on databases, power grids, and media. She could not recall any piece of intelligence that had promoted the idea that Russian elements might launch a physical attack on American assets abroad. "This is drastically different than anything I've seen."

"I agree. That's why I called. Jim and the Joint Chiefs have an ISIS stronghold in their sights."

"Are you telling me that they are recommending aggressive action against a group they don't believe is behind this plot."

"They can't be sure. The hope is to flush them out. It's likely that the SVR is embedded there, directing efforts."

Candace took a breath and processed the information.

"There's a window, Candy."

"I understand that. You've been dealing with this for eight years, Don. Technically, it's your call. What's your position?"

"Fifty-fifty," he admitted.

"That's helpful."

President Wallace chuckled. "Most of the time I find myself hovering in that range. It could go either way, Candy. The people they are targeting are targeting us one way or another."

"I understand that. This could be exactly what they want."

The president sighed. "It could."

Candace looked at the clock on the wall. "I have to leave in fifteen minutes, It's a ten-minute ride to St. John's. What are the chances we can loop Jim into a call in the next five minutes?"

"I'll speak to you in three."

Candace disconnected the call. "You have got to be kidding me."

⁕

"Where's Mom?" Marianne asked.

"She's in the other room on the phone?"

"Reviewing with Cassidy?" Marianne guessed.

"No."

"JD?"

"I don't know, Marianne. President Wallace called."

"Maybe he wanted to wish her well before you left."

"I don't think so."

⁕

"You have five minutes, Jim," Candace said. "Make your case."

Jim Bryce looked at the president. Wallace nodded. "We have a three-hour window. Anything beyond that and we risk losing our chance."

"Our chance to what?" Candace asked.

"To remove a terrorist cell in Brussels. State Security Service is on board so is MI6."

Candace sighed heavily. "I see. You believe that the SVR is behind this?"

"There's reason to believe that," Bryce replied.

"Behind the plan to attack our embassies?" Candace sought to clarify.

"There are SVR agents embedded in this cell. The intelligence came from MI6."

Candace let the information roll around in her brain for a moment. "What's their end game, Jim? The KGB wrote the playbook we all follow. What's the goal?"

"What do you mean?"

"If the intelligence you have is correct; if SVR agents have penetrated this cell and have been promoting this plot, what makes you think they didn't do it solely for you to get this information?"

"It's possible. These are not our friends."

"No, they are not," Candace agreed. "My concern is why the SVR would engineer this. Their reasons seldom lie on the surface. If you're right; something else is driving this. Don?"

"I agree."

"You want us to sit it out," Bryce guessed.

"I want you to get an asset in there," Candace said. "Our asset, not anyone else's."

"That might not be easy," Bryce replied.

"I don't expect it will be," Candace said. "Get someone on the inside. That's the best solution."

"They might move before we…"

"Then, I would suggest we move now."

President Wallace grinned. "It's a good plan, Jim."

"It's not that simple," Bryce said.

"If it was simple, everyone would make these decisions," Candace chimed. "I'm not prepared to play into Russia's hand. With that said, it remains President Wallace's call."

"I agree," Wallace said. "Unless you can provide something more concrete; we look to infiltrate and assess from there."

"MI6 is reliable," Bryce said.

Candace bit her lip. Reliable? Intelligence was only as reliable as the source. She'd spent hours with Alex and Jane covering this topic. Her discussions with her incoming National Security Adviser encompassed all these issues. Intelligence operatives were not only charged with gathering information about threats and the intentions of foreign governments. They were also tasked with planting disinformation. That meant that every bit of information received had to be vetted carefully.

"MI6 is not the CIA, Jim. It's not NSA. It's not DOD. Get me something I can use by the time I get to

The White House this morning. Otherwise, my position stands. I will respect President Wallace's decision, however."

"I'm in agreement," Wallace said. "You need to get to church," he said. "I'll see you shortly."

"I was looking forward to it," Candace joked.

"Welcome to the job," he replied. He turned to his Secretary of Defense. "She's right."

"It's not about right, Mr. President. Sometimes, it's about action."

Wallace nodded. "Sometimes it's about not reacting," he said. "Call Joshua Tate."

"That's not protocol."

"Since when does protocol dictate good sense? Call Tate. Apprise him. She needs everyone at the ready the moment I depart the Capitol."

"Yes, Sir."

Wallace let out a long sigh. The job of the president was never-ending. He hadn't humored Candace. Her questions and her recommendation were clear, concise, and sensible. He smiled. *She's ready.*

⚜

Jameson took Candace's hand when the door to the limousine closed. Candace had been quiet on the ride to St. John's Episcopal Church. It was obvious that something was on her mind. "Are you all right?"

"I am," Candace replied. She squeezed the hand in hers gently.

"What happened this morning?"

"Let's just say I got an early start."

"Anything I can help with?"

"Sometimes, Jameson, there are no good decisions to make. Outcomes are always unpredictable. I'm confident I made the best decision I could. That's all I can hope to do."

Jameson nodded. "I hope it didn't spoil today for you."

"Not at all," Candace said. "It reminded me what today is all about."

❦

Candace closed her eyes and took a deep breath as the car rolled through The White House gates. In a few hours, this would be her home. *Deep breath, Candy. Deep breath.*

Jameson leaned over to whisper in Candace's ear. This would be their last minute alone for many hours. After pictures with President and Mrs. Wallace, Candace would join the president while Jameson visited with Marion Wallace for a short time. They'd finish with coffee together. Candace would leave The White House with the outgoing president. Jameson would accompany the outgoing First Lady on the short trek.

From that point until they returned to this majestic place to get ready for the evening's events, Candace and Jameson would be surrounded by people. Everything they did, every gesture either made, every shared expression would be scrutinized by someone.

"I'm not sure when I'll get to say this again," Jameson said. "I love you more than anything, Candace—more than anything."

Candace took Jameson's face in her hands. Her eyes sparkled with affection and gratefulness. Her fingertip faintly traced Jameson's lips. "I love you," she promised with a gentle kiss. She wiped the corner of Jameson's lips with her thumb. "I always seem to leave something behind," she commented.

"More than lipstick," Jameson replied cheekily.

Candace shook her head.

Jameson shrugged and then laughed.

"What?" Candace asked as the car came to a stop.

"I was just thinking we have a unique advantage."

"Oh?"

"Yeah. Most couples have to get through this day without any alone time."

"Uh-huh…"

"Well, we use the same bathroom," Jameson explained. "You know, everyone expects women to go in pairs."

Candace fell into a fit of laughter. "You are a complete lunatic."

"That'll be First Lunatic, Madame President."

Candace continued to laugh softly. "I don't know what I'd do without you."

꽃

Joshua Tate entered the small conference room with the incoming Secretary of State, Jennifer Gorham, the incoming Secretary of Defense, Gil Rodgers, Secretary of Defense, Jim Bryce, President Wallace's National Security Adviser, Evan Shore, and the current Secretary of State, George Bennington. He measured the room as he always did, gauging the posture of Wallace's team. "I'll assume this isn't a party to celebrate," Tate surmised.

"Unfortunately, no," Bryce replied. "President Wallace and President-Elect Reid asked that we come together before today's ceremonies. Shortly, this will be placed in the new president's hands, and tomorrow in yours."

"We're listening," Jennifer Gorham said.

"This morning, I proposed a covert operation in Brussels aimed at a known ISIS cell that we have reason to believe is planning attacks on several diplomatic targets in Europe. The president and president-elect were both made aware of the intelligence we've received and concurred that at this time, the best course of action would entail placing an intelligence operative or operatives within the operation."

"You disagree," Tate guessed.

"It's not my place to agree or disagree, Director Tate. It's my responsibility to provide the information and my assessment of it. It's the president's job to decide how we proceed."

"But you have an opinion," Tate said.

"Placing someone will not be easy. Our MI6 contact spent four years infiltrating that cell."

"What was the president's reasoning?" Gil Rodgers inquired.

"It was the president-elect's recommendation. The president concurred," Bryce explained.

Rodgers was a former Rear Admiral who would formally replace Bryce the next day. He continued his questioning. "She had a reason. What was it?"

"There is evidence that the group may also have an SVR presence; one that may have greater influence than our allies," Bryce said.

Tate had to remind himself to remain stoic. He'd been entrenched in the spy game for more years than he cared to count. Little surprised him. When it involved the Russian Foreign Intelligence Service, he expected the unexpected. Without all the details, he regarded Candace's directive as prudent. In his experience, elected officials often lacked the ability to act rather than react. The intelligence world was a global chessboard full of self-appointed kings and queens, and pawns deluded into believing they were knights. It sounded horrible to say; it was horrible, but the fact remained that for most people involved in espionage, their work was their life, and their life was a high-stakes game. Money bought influence. Influence equated to power, and everyone involved had something to gain and something to lose in the equation. He understood the majority of Washingtonians had little if any concept of what happened in the underbelly of covert operations. The United States had no clear allies nor defined adversaries. Alliances were constantly shifting. The best defense was a strategic offense; one that employed savvy, loyal emissaries. Loyalty was a rare commodity. That is why Candace exercised caution.

Candace had been counseled by Alex Toles and Jane Merrow. In Tate's estimation, there were no two people with more first-hand knowledge of the inner-workings of the global intelligence community. The president-elect had clearly taken notes. He considered his response to the room. His career was public knowledge. He'd been an assistant director at the FBI, he'd worked at Treasury at FINCEN, and had spent the latter part of his career as Director of the National Security Agency. His law enforcement background was as well-rounded as it was well-known. Few people understood the knowledge he carried from those years. He too had worked off the grid. He leaned back in his chair and looked directly at Secretary Bryce.

"Who did the intelligence come from?" Tate asked.

"Our MI6 partner."

Tate nodded. "That's the source of the SVR intel as well?"

"It is. It's not a hundred-percent certainty," Bryce said.

Tate almost laughed. A hundred-percent certainty? Nothing ever rose to that level until an operation reached completion. "And, what is Russia's interest?"

"That's the perplexing piece," Bryce said.

Evan Shore entered the conversation. "It's a possible diversion."

Everything's a possible diversion. Tate nodded. "The question is whether an SVR agent's directive is to attack us physically. To use ISIS for that attack as a diversion or if they hope to divert us by convincing us an attack is imminent."

"That we can't say," Shore admitted.

Tate had spoken with Jane Merrow the previous day. He had taken a call from Alex Toles' brother, Jonathan Krause a week earlier. Krause remained deeply involved with international security at the Central Intelligence Agency. No mention had been made of any ISIS operations targeting diplomatic entities in Europe; at least, none that were credible. There was always the lone-wolf. ISIS tended to use the hand of young, impressionable men. They created zealots to carry out attacks. There was no question that they were organized, but they were not nearly as discerning as Russian intelligence operatives were. Tate suspected something was amiss. The intelligence was a house of cards; one that someone hoped would fall on Candace Reid as she took office.

"I'm sure I speak for all of us when I say we appreciate the heads up," Tate said.

"You agree with this course of action?" Shore asked his counterpart.

Tate shrugged. "You don't know what the agenda is. You're not operating in some cave in the deserts of Afghanistan, Evan. Everyone is paying attention to Europe."

"You think someone is throwing bait?" Evan Shore asked.

"It's possible. In my experience when you're dealing with more possibilities than probabilities, prudence is your ally," Tate said.

Shore nodded. "She's lucky to have you," he complimented the man who would play the role he had for three years.

"Not at all," Tate said. "It's my honor to serve her."

❧❧

"Sorry I had to make that call this morning," President Wallace apologized.

"Don't be. I appreciate the consideration."

"As far as I'm concerned, this is your ship to steer now, Candy."

"Let's hope I don't run into any icebergs on my first day."

Wallace grinned. "You rattled Bryce."

Candace was curious.

"He didn't expect you to take command," Wallace explained.

"I meant what I said, Don. This is still your call. This is still your home."

"Perhaps," he said. "I agree with your appraisal of the situation." He sipped from his coffee cup. "Shore and Bryce have your team in a conference room at the Capitol."

"That should be interesting."

"Tate was a smart choice."

"I think so."

"You're ready," Wallace said.

"Is anyone ready?" Candace retorted.

"No. You're more prepared than I was."

"I doubt that."

"Don't. Don't doubt it for a second. You are. If you need anything—an ear, a shoulder, a good bottle of scotch..."

Candace chuckled. "Be careful what you offer, Don."

"I'm a phone call away. I can't tell you how many times I wished I could bend John's ear."

Candace sobered. She missed John Merrow's friendship, his humor, and the way he could deconstruct a situation that demonstrated his perspicacity. She was grateful for the man seated across from her. Don Wallace was a thoughtful man of integrity. Candace was confident she would seek his counsel often.

"He would have loved to see this," she said. "You and me sitting in his old office sharing coffee before a changing of the guard. Two rusty old senators who managed to win the White House."

Wallace laughed. He got up from his chair and pulled a bottle of scotch from a cabinet. "I think this calls for a toast with something a little stronger."

"Before I take the oath?"

"It's tradition. Don't tell anyone."

Candace laughed. "Pour the scotch, Mr. President."

"Ready for the move?" Marion Wallace asked Jameson.

"I hope so. Cooper and Spencer were up at the crack of dawn," she said. "Wondering when they could go to the big white house."

Marion grinned. "It's been a while since this house had young children running through the halls on a daily basis."

"Oh, I'm sure Coop and Spence will make up for all that lost time. I know Cooper will miss him, though."

"It's one the hardest parts of the change," Marion observed. "It's not as if our children weren't already away at college when Don took office. It's not easy to travel at your leisure here. Balance is important, Jameson. No matter what, don't let Candace get lost in these hallways."

Jameson nodded.

"Don did his first few months here. He didn't sleep. He barely talked when he came to bed. Not because he couldn't share things. He was so afraid he would miss something, I think. Then he did." She sighed. "He missed Bridget's birthday."

Bridget was Don and Marion's youngest daughter. Jameson had met the Wallace children a handful of times. She would see them again shortly. She'd noticed that President Wallace seemed to have a close relationship with Bridget.

"Let me guess; he beat the hell out of himself."

"He did," Marion said. "Over and over for days. Bridget was eighteen. She took it in stride. He was the president. She was wrapped up in her new boyfriend." She laughed. "When he realized she wasn't all that devastated; he started coming back to the real world."

"I can't imagine it's easy dealing with what they have to all day and coming home as if it's perfectly normal."

"No, and that's why home needs to be normal, JD. As much as possible, let Cooper run through these halls. Encourage the kids to visit. Toast marshmallows, eat pizza; do the things you've always done. You'll never forget where you are. It's impossible. There are reminders everywhere. Make where you are home—for all of you. She'll need that more than she understands yet."

"The real role of the First Lady," Jameson said.

"It is," Marion agreed. "I think so. Shaking hands, Easter Egg hunts, interviews, answering mail, working with charities—it all matters. Nothing matters more than keeping the person you love steady."

Jameson nodded. "I think I understand."

Marion stood and took a deep breath. "Let's go find those two and make sure they haven't consumed that whole bottle of scotch in the corner cabinet."

"Scotch? At ten in the morning?"

"Probably the reason they instituted coffee as the formal festivity." Marion giggled. "A moment alone and a toast with a glass of scotch is a tradition none of us are supposed to know about," Marion explained. "There seem to be a lot of those. The problem is everyone from the cleaning staff to the press office knows before you will."

Jameson laughed. "Maybe it's time to create a few new ones."

Marion winked. "I can't wait to see what you come up with."

Jameson grinned. *Fortune cookies and Bible Study, oh, and fireplaces.*

CHAPTER TEN

Candace accepted a kiss on the cheek from Jameson. "I'll see you at the Capitol," she said.

"I'll be there unless there's a tradition of First Ladies hitting the drive-thru first," Jameson replied.

"I'm positive I don't want to know."

"See you shortly," Jameson said.

Candace buttoned her coat and looked at her predecessor. "Any chance you stowed that scotch in your jacket?"

"Looking for a little liquid courage?" Wallace asked.

"More like warmth. It's freezing."

"Believe me, you won't need the heaters when you get up there," the president advised. "The blood will be pumping so hard through your veins, you'll be able to heat the entire city."

Probably true. Candace followed President Wallace to the car, offered a wave to the press, and slid into her seat. *No turning back now, Candy.*

"Have you seen Mom yet?" Michelle asked Jonah.

"No. I heard someone say that JD's car just pulled in. They'll probably be here in a minute," Jonah replied. "Why are you freaking out?"

"Jonah, our mother is about to become the president."

"Yeah. I got that memo a couple of months back. She's still Mom."

"Yes, she is," Pearl sauntered up to the pair.

"Have you talked to her, Grandma?"

Pearl turned to Jonah. "Give us a minute."

"Good luck," he said.

"Care to tell me what this is all about?" Pearl asked.

"I don't know what you're talking about," Michelle answered.

"You've been fidgeting like there's a swarm of ants in your pants since we got here," Pearl observed.

Michelle didn't know how to respond. She hadn't given any thought to her nervousness. She'd been awake most of the night tossing and turning. Melanie finally got up and made her a cup of tea. She didn't seem to have any conscious thought, only emotions. She was excited. She was also suddenly terrified.

"Shell?" Pearl grabbed Michelle's arm.

"I don't know, Grandma. I can't believe it, I guess." She took a deep breath. "I can't believe she'll be gone, so will JD, and so will you."

Pearl smiled. "We're a phone call away."

"It's not the same."

"No," Pearl agreed. "She'll miss you more than you will have time to miss her with that colony you seem to be creating."

"Colony? I can't help that I had twins!"

Pearl sniggered. "And another on the way. Always trying to pull ahead of your sister and brother," she teased.

"I am not."

"If you say so."

Michelle sighed. "Mom won't have time to miss me."

Pearl shook her head. "Your mother is right."

"About what?"

"She always says this family needs an asylum. You are a lunatic if you believe that," Pearl said.

"I'm being selfish."

"No," Pearl disagreed.

Michelle was caught off guard by her grandmother's response.

Pearl smiled. "It's not selfish to wish you could keep her close, Shell. It'd be selfish to ask her not to go because you wish it." She caught a glimpse of Candace and Jameson heading toward the door beside President Wallace and the First Lady. "Don't look now," she said. "The chief loon is headed this way."

"Mommy!" Cooper ran for Candace.

"Hi, sweetheart." Candace accepted an exuberant hug from her youngest child.

"This place is big, Mommy."

Candace's smile lit her from within. Cooper's innocent excitement captured her heart. "It is big," she agreed. "You know, I used to work in this building."

Cooper's eyes opened wide. "You did?"

"I did," Candace told him.

"Mommy, you've had a lot of white houses."

Candace pulled Cooper close and laughed. "I suppose I have."

"Nana!" Spencer grabbed Candace around the waist.

"Hello, Spencer."

"You look important, Nana," he said. "Kinda like Mommy."

Candace struggled to keep a straight face. "Well, thank you," she replied. "And, you look handsome." She glanced over at Michelle who was trying to avoid her gaze.

"You did my tie," Spencer reminded her.

Candace frowned. "That must be why it's crooked." She winked. "Why don't you go ask Scott to help you straighten it?"

"Kay! Come on, Coop!"

"I'll see you both later," Candace promised. She made her way to Michelle.

"His tie isn't crooked," Michelle said.

"No."

"How come you sent him to Scott?" Michelle asked.

Candace pulled Michelle into a corner. She sighed. "I should've had you stay with us last night."

"What? Why?"

Candace placed her palm on Michelle's cheek. "I wouldn't be here without you, Shell. I hope you realize that because I do."

"Mom, I didn't..."

"You challenged me. Sometimes, I wanted to throttle you," Candace admitted. "It was good for me. Remember something," she said. "Whatever you decide you want to do a year, or two, or ten from now; you can do it. You're one of the most talented communicators I know."

"Mom..."

Candace winked. "Now, I need to find my wife."

Michelle rolled her eyes. "She's covered in kids."

Candace turned to find Jameson surrounded by Cooper, Spencer, JJ, and Nate Ellison's boys. "Maybe she's really Peter Pan."

"Could be. He built a whole world. Then again it was called Never Never Land."

Candace laughed. "Sounds about right."

"Mom," Jonah tugged on Candace's sleeve. "I think they're getting ready to start."

Candace nodded. "We'll talk later," she told Michelle. "I'm going to grab Jameson for a minute."

A voice called for the Ellison's children and Candace's family to head to the corridor that would lead them to the West Platform of the Capitol Building. Marianne corralled Spencer and Cooper. "Spencer," she said. "You need to go with Scott now."

"What about Coop?" Spencer asked.

"Remember, we talked about this? You and Maddie are going to go with Scott. Laura and Mel will be with you too."

"And, Grandma Maureen?"

Marianne nodded. "Grandma Maureen and Grandpa are going too."

"I have to leave Coop?"

Marianne took a deep breath and squatted to her son's height. "Today is Nana's big day. Cooper and I will see you outside in a few minutes, okay?"

Spencer shuffled his feet.

"Spencer, I know Cooper is like your brother. But Cooper is my brother," she reminded him. "He has to go with me, Jonah, and Shell. Okay? You can stand together when we get there, and you will be together all week."

Spencer nodded. He looked up at Jameson. "Jay Jay?"

"Yeah, buddy?"

"Will you come too?"

"I have to stand with Nana for a few minutes, but I promise; I will see you out there."

Spencer nodded.

"Go on," Marianne said.

"He could've walked with you if it meant that much to him," Jameson said.

Marianne smiled. Life in the Fletcher-Reid family was anything but ordinary. She suspected that Jameson would always regard Spencer more as a son than a grandson, just as Spencer thought of Cooper as a brother, not an uncle. "It's good for him to learn he can't always get his way," she said. "Besides, Cooper is your son. He deserves that spotlight today."

"So, do you," Jameson said.

Marianne offered her hand to Cooper. "Come on," she said. "Give Momma a hug and lets you and me make sure Jonah's tie is straight."

Cooper hugged Jameson hard.

"Keep your sisters in line," Jameson said.

Cooper giggled. "And Jonah."

"And Jonah," Jameson agreed. She took a deep breath and made her way across the room to Candace. "Any last words?"

Candace laughed. "I don't know. Got any fortune cookies?"

Jameson's eyes twinkled.

"No..."

Jameson reached into her jacket pocket and pulled out a fortune cookie. "Thought you might like a glimpse of the future."

Candace held Jameson's gaze as she cracked open the cookie.

"Well?" Jameson asked. "Aren't you going to read it before they herd us like cattle?"

Candace snickered and dropped her eyes to the slip of paper between her fingers. *"The best is yet to come."* She looked back at Jameson. She often wondered how many of these special cookies Jameson kept hidden. It didn't matter. Jameson understood that Candace's penchant for Chinese take-out and a cabinet of fortune cookies was rooted in a need for simple pleasures. In their way, the folding containers and the cookies filled with silly phrases, proverbs, and romantic sentiments reminded Candace that meaning in life was found moment to moment. Caviar and champagne had their place. Chicken wings and cookies in plastic wrappers equated to home, to the people who had nurtured Candace as a child. Candace hoped to instill the same sense of purpose, hopefulness, and wonderment in her children and grandchildren that her grandparents and Pearl had engendered in her. It seemed like a little thing. It wasn't. Jameson's fortune cookies were nothing short of a love letter—each and every one.

"Mrs. Wallace and Ms. Reid," a voice called into the holding room.

"That's me," Jameson said.

"Jameson." Candace pulled Jameson back. "Make sure you add 'in bed' to that one," she whispered.

"Where do you think I got the fireplace idea?" Jameson kissed Candace's cheek.

"She's something else," President Wallace said.

"You have no idea, Don; no idea at all."

❦

Jameson offered Janine Ellison a smile. "Are you ready for this?"

"Between you and me? Not even a little bit."

"Nate is good for Candace. They make a good team."

"I think so," Janine agreed. "What about you? I barely got to talk to you this morning at coffee. How are you holding up?"

"I just can't wait to see her walk onto the platform," Jameson said.

"I understand," Janine replied.

Jameson looked over her shoulder to where Nate Ellison was standing a short way behind them with his entourage. Ahead, she could see Jonah leaning into Michelle's ear. In her wildest childhood dreams, she would never have imagined standing in this hallway. She was grateful that she would arrive on the West Platform before Candace. She would have the chance to watch Candace enter. The group ahead pulled out of sight. Jameson took a deep breath. "Here we go."

❦

Michelle looked out at the crowd as they waited to be announced. "Oh, my God."

"Senator Blake told me they estimate the crowd at about 1.5 million," Jonah said.

Cooper tugged on Marianne's hand. "A million is a lot."

"Mom is a popular lady, Coop," Marianne said.

Cooper beamed. "She's ours," he said. "And Momma's."

Marianne heard Pearl chuckle. "Yes, she is, Cooper. Yes, she is."

⁓⁕⁓

Candace weaved through a small cluster of people and embraced Nate Ellison. "Thank you for taking this journey with me."

The future vice president smiled warmly. "Thank you for giving me the chance."

"I'll see you on the other side," Candace said.

⁓⁕⁓

Cooper held Marianne's hand tightly.

"It's okay, Coop," she whispered. "Your momma's next."

"Ladies and gentlemen," the announcer began. "Ms. Jameson Reid and Mrs. Janine Ellison accompanied by Secretary of the Senate Danielle Pierce and...."

"See?" Marianne whispered. "There she is."

"JD looks excited," Jonah commented.

"Aren't you?" Laura whispered.

꿍꿍

Jameson failed to understand people's excitement about her arrival to anything. Her entire claim to fame was loving Candace. That was it from her point of view. She started down the stairs, acknowledging a few familiar faces with an offered hand or a nod. How many people were watching? She forced herself not to think about the sea of faces standing in front of the Capitol. Candace might have had her detractors; she had far more supporters. Who wouldn't want to share a piece of history; to say they were there the day the first woman became President of the United States? She moved across the aisle to embrace Marion Wallace.

"Good luck, JD," Marion said.

"Think I'll need it?" Jameson whispered.

"I left you a little something," Marion replied. "Look in the recreation room upstairs."

Jameson nodded and made her way to her family. Cooper immediately fell to her side. She bent over and spoke to him softly. "I know there are a lot of people, buddy. Just remember that Mommy and I love you more than anything; okay?"

He nodded. Jameson took his hand and looked at Pearl.

Pearl's eyes were riveted to the door Candace would walk through; waiting impatiently to see the daughter she loved come into view.

Jameson followed Pearl's gaze upward as the current president and vice president entered. Within seconds, both had offered her a kiss on the cheek. President Wallace leaned into her ear. "I left the president a few take-out menus."

Of all the things the millions of people watching might guess President Wallace said to conjure Jameson's laughter, she was confident take-out menus would not be on anyone's list. She shook her head with amusement as the president crossed the platform to his family. She'd been so busy musing about the president's humor, she'd completely tuned out Nate Ellison's introduction. She had to mentally shake herself back to reality when he embraced her.

Jameson took a deep breath. *This is it.*

゛ヿ゛ヾ

Candace smiled at several familiar faces and nodded her thanks for their congratulatory wishes. Already, all eyes were on her. She could feel them near and far waiting to see what she would say to them. She slowed her breathing, hoping it might tame the fierce pounding of her heart. A swishing sound she identified as the blood moving through her veins whirled in her ears. She'd experienced profound moments in her life; the birth of her children, the loss of her sons, the death of her parents, the moment she realized she had fallen in love with Jameson, the day they brought Cooper home — all of those moments had stolen the air from her lungs with their gravity. Today did not eclipse any of the seminal moments in Candace's life. It was, she thought, the culmination of all of those experiences that led her here. It was seeing the potential in new life. It was understanding the palpable sadness that came with loss. It was experiencing the foundation love provided. She carried each of those moments, every person who touched her life and her heart over a lifetime with her today. She heard a chorus of horns herald her introduction. With a deep breath, she offered a silent prayer. "God, watch over me as I do my best to watch over all of them."

"Ladies and gentlemen, the president-elect of the United States, Candace Stratton Reid."

Jameson's eyes fixed on the doorway. *Candace.* "I love you." The words fell from her without reservation or permission. She felt Marianne's hand press into the small of her back in support. The thought passed through her mind that Candace looked regal as she stepped through the opening that led to the West Platform. Candace turned and accepted the well-wishes of several friends and dignitaries as she descended the stairs. Her posture exuded confidence and resolve without appearing rigid. Jameson marveled at her wife's composure. Watching Candace as she approached, Jameson feared she might lose the ability to stand.

Marianne stepped a touch closer, sensing Jameson's wavering. "She is amazing," Marianne commented.

"She's everything," Jameson said.

⚜

Candace's eyes met Jameson's when she reached the bottom of the stairs. Amid the thunderous roar of the crowd, her world went silent. Jameson's smile calmed the beating of her heart, speaking without words, anchoring her in the safe harbor Jameson had created in her life. She accepted a silent kiss on the cheek from her wife. No words were needed. She bent over and embraced Cooper, then proceeded to offer each of her grown children an affectionate hug. A peck on Janine Ellison's cheek was followed by an embrace from Nate Ellison. "No turning back," she whispered.

"Wouldn't dream of it," he said.

Candace crossed the aisle and smiled at President Wallace. He leaned into her ear. "Breathe," he advised.

Candace finished with the necessary pleasantries and stood beside the vice-president elect. She allowed herself to look out at the crowd for the first time. *Dear God.* She repeated her silent prayer, hoping someone was listening. People were counting on her to raise their hopes and to elevate their opportunity. She would need guidance and strength to deliver. *If you're listening, please give me the strength.*

※ ※ ※

Only a few minutes had passed as the children's chorus began its rendition of America the Beautiful. Candace had made it clear that she didn't want her inauguration burgeoning with celebrities. There would be a poem from an award-winning poet, and one of Candace's greatest advocates, Karla Reiff, a popular Broadway actress would sing a medley. There was no way to avoid the spectacle of this day. Candace desired that it reflect the sea of people below more than it celebrated those seated above. Jameson had listened to Candace's end of several conversations on the subject. Even Dana had warned that people might perceive Candace's reluctance to invite celebrities as evidence of a fear her star might be eclipsed. Candace had scoffed at the notion. Jameson's brain tuned out the sights and sounds around her as she replayed Candace's words.

"Contrary to what you all keep telling me, it is not my day. It's the day we peacefully transfer power. It's as much President Wallace's day and a day for every person who votes as it is for me. That is what it will reflect."

A smile curled Jameson's lips. Sitting behind Candace, she could not see the expression on her wife's face. She didn't need to. Candace was thinking about the people looking up to her, not just literally but metaphorically. That is why Candace sat in the seat she now occupied. Jameson allowed herself to return to the present, still wondering how a few minutes could feel like a lifetime.

⚜

Candace hugged Nate Ellison as he stepped back from taking his oath. "Congratulations, Mr. Vice President."

"I won't let you down," he said.

Candace smiled. "I know."

⚜

"I can't watch it."

Petru Rusnac laughed. "Shut it off."

"I can't look away."

"Lawson, are you in love with Candace Reid?"

"What the hell are you talking about?"

Rusnac laughed heartily and took a sip of his drink. "You're obsessed with the woman."

"She threatens everything."

"Ah, where there are challenges, Lawson, there are also opportunities. Look at your daughter."

Klein threw his glass across the room. "Don't talk about my daughter."

Rusnac laughed harder and shook his head. "Waste of good scotch, Lawson."

"Fuck you."

Rusnac moved closer to Klein's chair. "Be careful, Lawson. People might get the wrong idea about you."

Klein bristled and returned his focus to the television, unable to look away.

✺

Candace stood and walked a few steps toward the podium. Jameson stepped beside her and held John Merrow's Bible in her hands. Marianne stood beside Jameson with Cooper in front of her and Michelle and Jonah to her side. She took a deep breath as the Chief

Justice of the Supreme Court, William Biel addressed her.

"Governor Reid, are you prepared to take the oath?"

"I am."

"Would you please raise your right hand and repeat after me."

Candace placed her left hand on the Bible that Jameson held, and raised her right as instructed.

Justice Biel began. "I, Candace Stratton Reid do solemnly swear."

"I, Candace Stratton Reid do solemnly swear."

"That I will faithfully execute the office of President of the United States."

Candace took a breath. "That I will faithfully execute the office of President of the United States."

Michelle's hand fell into Marianne's. Marianne gripped Cooper's shoulder.

"And will to the best of my ability," Justice Biel continued.

"And will to the best of my ability."

"Preserve, protect, and defend the Constitution of the United States."

Candace repeated the words confidently. "Preserve, protect, and defend the Constitution of the United States."

"So, help me, God."

"So, help me, God," Candace said.

Justice Biel smiled. "Congratulations, Madame President."

Candace let out the breath she'd been holding. She shook the Chief Justice's hand. "Thank you."

The Marine Band began to play *All Hail the Chief.* She turned to Jameson. Tears glistened in Jameson's eyes. She kissed Jameson's lips lightly.

"I'm so proud of you," Jameson said.

Candace nodded, unable to speak. One shared word with Jameson and she feared her emotions might take hold of her. She bent over and held Cooper close for a moment. "I love you, sweetheart." She squeezed him tightly as a cannon salute began in the distance.

Cooper beamed with pride. He didn't fully understand the meaning of what had just occurred. The steady rumble of applause and shouts of congratulations weren't unfamiliar. The tears that gathered in his momma's and in his sisters' eyes were those of pride and affection. That much he did understand. That made him proud; proud of the mother he adored, and proud to be part of his family.

"Congratulations, Mom," Marianne said with a kiss.

"You did it," Michelle offered.

"We did," Candace corrected her.

"I can't believe my mom is the president," Jonah whispered. "I love you, Mom."

"I love you too," Candace said.

She shook a few more hands, hugged the former president again and finally turned to offer the crowd a wave. She smiled brightly, wishing she could see the faces attached to the millions of hands clapping and waving. No one could prepare for a moment like this. Candace didn't think there was an adjective to attach to the moment. So, few people had stood here. Pride, gratefulness, excitement all swelled within her; all of it reminding her that this was a moment for sobriety. This was a day of celebration. It marked a new beginning for Candace and for the country. How many prayers could she offer in the space of a few hours? As she waved, she again asked for guidance from above to help her remain resilient and grounded as she accepted the task before her. Who was she? She was only a woman who had loved, lost, struggled, worked, questioned, and hopefully, who tried to better herself each day. But Candace was only human. Standing on this platform, she realized that for all their deeds and words, the monuments erected across this city to those who stood here before her represented men—just men, not gods. Every person who had taken the oath she just had, had been fallible, hopeful, even misguided at times. She hoped they might be watching too, and in some way stand beside her as she promised to walk the path they had laid while carving a new landscape for the future. She offered the crowd another wave of acknowledgment, hoping they understood her sentiment — *I see you.* She stepped back to stand beside Vice President Ellison.

Senator Debbie Monroe made her way to the platform amid the continued rumble of an enthusiastic crowd. "I am humbled and honored to introduce to you the forty-fifth President of these United States, Candace Reid."

Candace thanked the senator as she passed and took her place before the nation.

"Candace, Candace, Candace," the crowd chanted the president's name as they had for months on the campaign trail.

"Thank you," Candace said. She waited a beat for the crowd to quiet and took a deep breath.

"My Fellow Americans,

Today marks a new day in American history, not because I stand before you; because each day provides us an opportunity to move forward. I want to thank President Wallace for his dedication and service to this wonderful country we share. And, I want to thank him for his partnership and leadership as we participate in the peaceful transition of power this nation has engaged in since its founding.

Each time a person has laid his or now, her hand on the Bible and taken the presidential oath, our country has faced obstacles. Change is constant in our world. It provides humanity a chance for growth. It also presents challenges that, at times, seem daunting. The story of America is not one of the few who seek and hold the highest office in the land, nor is it simply a tale of those who have toiled to build the railways, roads, and bridges we travel daily. It is a story of how Americans come together to serve the ideals set forth by our forefathers and foremothers, and the institutions they created. Institutions that we have endeavored to preserve for more than two centuries. And, endeavor to preserve them we must — together.

America, like every corner of the world, is no longer isolated. Gone are the days when the messages leaders deliver are carried by horseback. The crackle of radios is a distant memory to most. As I speak to you now, the world is listening. My words, our actions, the sights and sentiments that America offers are experienced by billions of people across the globe. And, for all our fallibility and faltering; millions still dream of crossing oceans, climbing mountains, and toiling through deserts to reach our shores. It has always been and will always be our commitment to building a prosperous society that seeks greater equality and understanding that captivates the human imagination. It is our ability to thrive in our diversity that makes America a beacon of light in the world.

But prosperity has eluded far too many of our fellow citizens. Where we once built roads and bridges, skyscrapers, and submarines, we now find crumbling factories and declining steel mills. As technology has advanced, the landscape for American prosperity has too often failed to keep pace. We must revitalize our efforts to build anew. The superhighway of the internet cannot take precedence over the roads that carry us across an expansive nation or the airports and harbors that provide our gateway to the world beyond our borders. Our economy can only thrive when we invest in creation; the creation of new technology in partnership with tried and true methods to build and produce the finest materials and infrastructure in the world. We can do it. Americans possess the ingenuity and the tenacity to accomplish anything we set our minds to.

Too often, we romanticize the past or dream only of the future. Yesterday is our teacher. It instructs us and reminds us where we have triumphed and where we have fallen short. Tomorrow is not promised to any of us, yet it inspires our actions today. Today is where we live. We cannot remain content to walk only in the footsteps of our parents and grandparents. We must forge new paths. We are stewards of the planet we share. We are the guardians of our fate. Preserving our planet's health, promoting the health of our society must be and will be paramount in our effort to create a brighter tomorrow. Industry and government, schools, our many houses of worship, and our kitchen tables all must participate in this endeavor. Few things threaten our security more than the declining health of our planet and its people.

There will be cynics; those who believe that government has no interest in the people it is meant to serve. There is reason to be cynical at times. Those who seek to serve in the halls of power must be steeped in both confidence and humility. I, like those who serve beside me, have been entrusted with your care. It is in our best interest to work toward consensus rather than to immerse ourselves in conflict, to seek to do what is best rather than to prove we are right.

We cannot lose sight of those who, at this moment, traverse the most dangerous parts of our world to keep us safe at home; the soldiers, airmen, and sailors who sacrifice personal freedoms, and willingly risk their lives that we may enjoy the rights and privileges America bestows upon us.

We must commit to the care of the men and women who dedicate their talent, their time, and often their lives to the defense of our nation. We must, and we will ensure that they are equipped with the finest technology and resources available. The pinning of medals and the rhetoric of glory pales in the light of a country that does not provide for the needs of its military. Grateful sentiment is not a substitute for the provision of resources to the men and women who serve in our military. We entrust our protection to our servicemen and women. We can do no less than promise them the best healthcare, emotional support, and educational opportunities available.

The world is not without its dangers. There are those who will seek to do us harm. We have combatted fascism and communism. We have faced terrorists with a steely resolve and refused to allow their misguided ideology to inform our way of life. Throughout our history, we have overcome those who have sought to undermine our ideals. We have, and we will use every means at our disposal to ensure that America endures. Our goal has always been to achieve peace. Ironically, that mission has often led us to war.

Tanks and missiles, bombs and guns alone cannot pave the way to peace. Diplomacy, steady resolve, investing in old alliances and building new bridges will provide the cornerstones of peace. In times of peril and uncertainty, people often speak of walls and fences. There is no wall that cannot be scaled, no fence that cannot be climbed. We are better served by bridges, mindful that bridges and walls share one thing in common; without our care both will crumble.

In this new, global world, the frontlines of peace will not always come in the form of barbed wire. Technology and communication have changed the requirements for securing our nation. We must speak, act, and engage thoughtfully while never yielding to the threats of those who determine to undermine our democracy.

We are a nation of immigrants. We represent the world as a whole. Our culture is rich because of it, and we must remember our roots as we water our garden. We are black and white, brown and yellow, red and every shade in between. We worship in temples, churches, mosques, homes, and nature. We do not all look the same. We do not all speak the same language.

We do not all love the same. We do not all vote for the same people. Same is not what America has ever been. We have struggled with our diversity. Men and women have marched, fought, risked their livelihoods and their personhood so that we may enjoy a nation in which we are allowed equal opportunity. We cannot turn the page backward. We must write a new chapter, seeking greater understanding. What seems to divide us provides our greatest hope for the future. Every parent wishes a healthy, happy future for his or her child. Every child desires a parent that will be nurturing and accepting.

We begin to peel away the layers of prejudice when we close our eyes and listen. Each of us is a leader. Leadership does not require a proclamation, promotion or an election. Parents, teachers, pastors, doctors, lawyers, law enforcement, judges, Congress, no matter where we sit, we must commit to listen to each other as much as we speak.

Strengthening communities through education and economic revitalization is the key to diminishing bias. Only by investing in each other can we all climb higher. Our community is no longer defined by street signs. It encompasses continents.

To our neighbors, rich and poor, struggling and soaring, we promise to offer our hand to you in partnership. Indifference to suffering, whether around the block or across the world cannot be tolerated. Indifference leads to intolerance. A peaceful, hopeful world depends on those who enjoy the greatest benefits showing generosity and compassion. America, along with its allies must lead by example.

America was forged through revolution; a revolution not only fought in the forests of colonies but also imbued in the human spirit. Today we renew our commitment to the principles of equality and justice that our forebearers set forth. We resolve ourselves to cast aside the politics of divisiveness and vindictiveness. Americans are explorers. We are creators. We are the architects of our destiny.

Theodore Roosevelt, when he addressed a hopeful nation on the day of his inauguration said this: "They did their work, they left us the splendid heritage we now enjoy. We in our turn have an assured confidence that we shall be able to leave this heritage unwasted and enlarged to our children and our children's children. To do so we must show, not merely in great crises, but in the everyday affairs of life, the qualities of practical intelligence, of courage, of hardihood, and endurance, and above all the power of devotion to a lofty ideal."

Now, we go forward together with conscience and commitment to that lofty ideal; knowing that it will continue to inspire generations to come. We will be judged by more than our words. We will be measured by our deeds. Let us go now with grace and humility, confidence and compassion, and dedication to this shining city upon a hill we call America. Thank you all for your courage, commitment, and your love for this great nation. God Bless you, and God Bless the United States of America."

A renewed chorus of cheers and chants greeted Candace's ears. She waved to the people spread across the National Mall. The Washington Monument towered in the distance, another reminder of the gravity of this moment. For the first time, she heard herself acknowledge reality. *I'm the President of the United States.*

CHAPTER ELEVEN

Long days were something Candace and Jameson had grown accustomed to. Until now, Jameson had thought the day of the presidential election had been the longest in recorded history — until now.

"Tired?" Candace asked.

"Does it seem to you that today has lasted a week already?"

"Only a week?"

"Not that I don't love parades," Jameson said.

"I know; it's cold."

"Cold enough that we could be getting a head-start on our tour of The White House's fireplaces."

Candace laughed. "Behave, and I'll buy you a balloon."

"Is that part of protocol?"

"I don't know. It should be," Candace replied.

"Can I ask for one favor before we get out of this nice, warm car and walk?"

Candace raised her brow.

"Can I kiss the president?"

Candace smiled. "No. You can kiss your wife."

Jameson's lips met Candace's with a grateful kiss. "Are you sure we can't skip straight to the fireplaces?"

"Don't tempt me," Candace said. She pulled away with a deep breath. "Ready?"

Jameson nodded. She followed Candace out of the car. They would make the rest of the trek to their new home on foot, waving to the people who lined the streets in hopes of catching a glimpse of the new president. Jameson chuckled softly at the constant call of Candace's name.

Candace moved closer. "What's funny?"

"I was just wondering how many of them would like to take that fireplace tour with you."

Candace laughed. "Lunatic." She took Jameson's hand and waved with her other as they walked. *And, I'll bet at least half would prefer you were their guide.*

⚜

Candace surprised Jameson when they arrived at their new home. She started to make her way in the opposite direction from Jameson. It wasn't the surprise that Jameson hoped for.

"Where are you going?" Jameson asked. "The president's bedroom is this way. That's *our* bedroom."

"Yes, I know."

"What am I missing?"

"Well," Candace took a step closer. "Since you have decided to surprise me with the song we're dancing to at the Diversity Ball, I have decided that I want to surprise you."

"Surprise me?"

"Yes."

"With?"

"You will see me when we meet downstairs to leave."

Jameson was stunned. "You can't be serious."

"You know," Candace said. "We didn't do things traditionally when we got married."

"And?"

"I didn't sleep apart from you. You didn't watch me walk down an aisle. We've done everything in our life together—everything. I wouldn't change that. You do things for me all the time, Jameson. Things like handing me a fortune cookie before I'm about to become the president. Things like sending Chinese food to my Senate office. At every turn, you always know what to do when I need it, even when I don't know what I need."

"Candace…"

"I know that when I hear the song you've chosen, I'll lose my breath. I know it. I just want that chance, Jameson—tonight, I want to see your face when I walk into the room."

"You don't need to do anything to take my breath away, Candace."

Candace kissed Jameson lovingly. "It's only an hour or so."

"That's an eternity," Jameson said.

"Hopefully, I'll be worth the wait." Candace kissed Jameson again and headed down the hall.

"You're always worth the wait," Jameson called after her. She groaned. She loved to watch Candace get ready whether it was in the morning for work, at night for bed, or preparing for a formal event. Jameson had been looking forward to a few moments alone with Candace. She'd fantasized that she'd help Candace zip her dress and take the opportunity to touch her wife's skin sensually. All day, Jameson had been fighting the urge to pull Candace into her arms and kiss her passionately. She wanted a moment to hold Candace. An hour wasn't long; it would be hell.

⁂

"She's going to flip when she sees you," Marianne said.

"I hope so."

"I don't think you need to worry, Mom."

"She's seen me in a gown before."

"Not in *that* gown."

"You like it?"

Marianne wanted to laugh. Here stood the President of the United States in The White House, dressed in what Marianne thought was the most stunning navy-blue dress she'd ever seen, worrying whether

Jameson, of all people, would be impressed. Candace could walk into a room wearing a smock and Jameson would need support to keep from falling over. She had the advantage of watching her mother and Jameson from a distance. When Candace had first met Jameson, Marianne had feared their relationship might fade from infatuation to nothingness. Years later, she was sure that would never come to pass. It never mattered what was happening; Jameson always looked at Candace as if Candace were the greatest gift in the world. And, Candace's gaze never strayed far from Jameson when they were together. The connection they shared was undeniable to anyone who had the privilege to spend time with them. If Marianne envied anything in her mother's life, it was the way Jameson looked at Candace the moment she entered a room.

"I love the dress," Marianne said.

Candace's hopeful gaze was tinted with insecurity.

"She won't be looking at the dress," Marianne said.

Candace chuckled nervously. "I want tonight to be special for her."

"Mom," Marianne took her mother's hand. "She nearly went to her knees when you stepped onto the platform this morning.

Candace listened with interest.

"We all know how much you love JD," Marianne said. "You can't see the way she looks at you when you're not paying attention. You don't need to do anything to make today special for JD."

Candace forced her surfacing tears into submission. "Marianne," she began and stopped to take a breath. "I love you. God knows, I love you kids with all my heart."

Marianne smiled, sensing what her mother was about to say.

"Jameson is the love of my life. I thought I knew what that meant. This afternoon after you took Cooper into the hallway…"

"What?"

"She handed me a fortune cookie."

Marianne laughed. "I'm not surprised. I think she has a stash somewhere."

Candace nodded. "There were five words on the paper—just five; *the best is yet to come.* No one knows me like Jameson does. Sometimes, I still can't believe it. And, sometimes, Marianne, I wonder if I will ever be able to give her what she's given me."

"Well, I can't speak *for* JD. She is my best friend."

Candace smiled. Few things moved her as much as watching Jameson and Marianne's friendship blossom.

Marianne considered whether she should share what was on her mind with her mother. Jameson had become her closest friend. They shared many things in confidence. She was inclined to think Jameson would want Candace to know. "Before you left to come back here to DC," Marianne began. "JD told me something."

"What?"

Marianne searched her mother's eyes before continuing. She witnessed all the emotions she would expect. One thing Marianne understood; her mother never wanted Jameson to feel that anything was more important to her than their marriage, not even the presidency. Jameson would understand why she had decided to tell Candace. "She told me that she met with Shell's fertility specialist."

Candace was shocked.

"She wouldn't tell you this before the inauguration."

"Tell me what?"

"She can't get pregnant, Mom. She didn't want you to worry about her—not now."

Candace's eyes closed. *Jameson.*

"No one knows except me. She's planning to tell you next week."

Candace sighed. "That's why she said she didn't think having a baby was our path."

"She loves you, Mom. I know you know that. You don't have to worry about making anything special for JD. What makes her happy is seeing you happy. Today is special for her because she loves you. I didn't tell you this to upset you," Marianne said. "When JD told me, she said what hurt her the most was that you'd given her everything. She said that when you two talked about having children, she could tell the biggest part of you was hoping she'd say she wanted to have a baby. And, she did, Mom. She didn't know if she could yet.

She," Marianne stooped and took a breath. "JD said that she never thought about having a family until she met you."

"I know that."

"Yes, but she also said that you gave her something she can't give you."

Candace tightened her grip on Marianne's hands. "Thank you for telling me."

Marianne nodded. "You don't need to surprise her with anything. Can I tell you one more thing?"

Candace nodded.

"You both need to stop worrying that you don't give enough. I mean it. I'll tell you what I told her. Stop thinking that you aren't enough for her. You're everything to her. She said it herself today when you stepped onto the platform."

"Thank you," Candace said. She hugged her daughter. "For everything."

"No, Mom, thank you."

Jameson looked at her reflection. "I hope I did okay."

"I'd say you did better than okay," Pearl's voice offered.

Jameson spun on her heels.

"You look like the canary the cat caught." Pearl chuckled.

"Do you think this is okay?" Jameson looked down at her dress.

"Jameson, you look beautiful."

Jameson's nervousness was palpable.

"Why are you so nervous? It's not as if you haven't danced with Candy at a ball before."

"It's not the same."

"Worried about what the masses will think?" Pearl teased.

"No, only the president."

Pearl nodded. She took Jameson's hand and led her to sit on a sofa in the room. "The only person Candy will see the moment you walk into the room is you. That's it. Trust me on that one, Jameson."

"I want today to be the best day of her life — all of it."

"That's not going to happen."

Jameson sighed.

Pearl grinned. "It won't happen because she's already had the best day of her life — a few times over — and there will be more to come. Isn't that why you gave her that fortune today? To remind her of that; that there is a tomorrow?"

"How did you..."

"She showed me when we got here. I don't think you know how much that meant to her."

"I love her so much, Pearl."

"I know you do. She loves you too, you fool. I think she has since the day you showed up at the door."

"I don't think…"

"Oh, sometimes it happens. I think it happens more than most of us want to admit. It takes a little time for most of us to accept that it has happened; that we've lost our heart. I will tell you this; Candy changed after that day. She laughed more than I'd seen in years. There's a lightness to her that I thought might've disappeared forever. That's why she's made it this far, Jameson. She knows that. Don't you forget it."

Jameson hugged Pearl. "Thanks."

"So? What song *did* you choose?"

Jameson laughed. "I don't believe it; she sent you on a reconnaissance mission."

Pearl shrugged. "It was worth a try."

Jameson shook her head.

"I meant what I said, Jameson."

"I know."

"Don't forget it." Pearl got up. "Now, go meet Cinderella and take her to that ball."

❦

Jameson was engaged in a conversation with Marianne when Candace walked into the room. Marianne's gaze drifted over Jameson's shoulder. Jameson turned slowly. *Candace.* The hammering in her chest almost knocked her over.

Candace smiled at her wife.

Oh, my God. Jameson's eyes swept over Candace. The dress Candace wore was simple and elegant. The only thing preventing it from touching the floor were the heels that added an inch or two to Candace's height. The material cascaded over Candace's curves perfectly and the deep blue color made her eyes appear a shade darker. Candace's hair was swept up, leaving several curled tendrils to fall next to her face. A pearl choker was draped around her neck, highlighting the scoop that gave the faintest hint of Candace's cleavage. Subtle could be exquisite. Jameson held her breath as Candace closed the distance between them.

"Not as low-cut as you'd hoped?" Candace teased.

Jameson's heart was so full, she found it difficult to speak. Her eyes searched Candace's endlessly.

"You look amazing," Candace said. She stepped back and looked at Jameson again. Jameson's dress appeared almost silver in the light. Jameson seldom wore dresses. The few times that Candace had seen her wife in a gown, she'd been left speechless. As much as Jameson liked to joke about her tool belt, her aversion to any shoe that left the ground, and her confusion over why people found coloring their eyelids a good idea; she could pull off an evening gown as well as any movie star Candace had ever seen.

Jameson forgot that anyone else was in the room. She took Candace's face in her hands. "Do you have any idea how beautiful you are?"

Candace barely had the chance to smile before Jameson's lips found hers. "Does that mean you approve?" Candace asked.

"You are stunning." Jameson offered Candace her hand.

"Ready to go to the ball?" Candace asked.

"As long as no frisky senators try to fill your dance card."

"That's already been filled."

"Oh?"

"Apparently, it's first come, first serve. I assume that's why it says First Lady."

Jameson laughed. "And, you call me a lunatic?"

"First Lunatic." Candace winked. She grasped Jameson's hand. "Let's go."

"After you, Madame President."

Candace shook her head. "No, together."

❦

Jameson held Candace's hand on the short drive to the Diversity Ball. Her thumb continually caressed the skin beneath it. She'd yet to succeed in slowing the frantic pace of her heart. How it was possible to fall in love with someone over and over again, Jameson couldn't say. She felt as though she had fallen in love all over again; thrown off balance by the ferocity of emotion pounding through her body — another contradiction. Candace's presence could send Jameson's world spinning out of control. The moment that Jameson feared she would lose herself, Candace would find her and pull her close. Sometimes it was with nothing more than a glance. Jameson mused as the car rolled to a stop, that the secret to sustaining a marriage was finding ways to fall in love again and again.

"What's going on up there?" Candace asked Jameson.

Jameson's only reply was a smile. Her door opened. She stepped out and offered Candace her hand.

"Madame President," Secret Service Agent Blake Everson said. "This way."

"Thank you, Blake," Candace said. She walked in silence with Jameson as they navigated through a long corridor with their entourage. Their family had made their way to the ballroom ahead of their arrival. First, Candace and Jameson had stopped to meet with Nate and Janine Ellison who were also making the rounds to each of the ten official Inaugural Balls. Candace had chosen the Diversity Ball as their first stop, believing that it reflected the spirit of her campaign. From here they would wind their way around the city attending The New York Ball, The Youth Ball, The Community Ball, The Western States Ball, The Southern

States Ball, The Commander in Chief Ball, The Eastern
States Ball, The Midwestern Ball, and finally The Arts
and Culture Ball. Each stop would entail a few brief
remarks to the crowd from them both and a dance.
Most of the family would head home after the first appearance. Pearl and Marianne had offered to head back
to the townhouse with the kids so that Michelle,
Melanie, Jonah and Laura, and Jameson's parents could
enjoy the evening festivities to their fullest. It would be
a long night. It was also a night that Jameson had been
looking forward to. She was eager to be alone with
Candace, but she reveled in watching Candace command a stage. People were excited to see Candace step
up to the microphone in her gown and wave. It added
to the magic of the day. Jameson had come to understand that the pomp and circumstance had a purpose;
it engaged people and it left them feeling hopeful.
Hope was no small thing. Hope and excitement would
be needed to carry Candace's agenda. Jameson understood that.

She felt Candace's grip tighten as they rounded
a corner. The steady beat of music drummed in Jameson's ears. Excitement took over. Now, she would get to
give Candace her surprise. She'd spent days listening
to songs that reminded her of Candace, songs Candace
loved, songs they had listened to and made love to,
songs that inspired her—hundreds she guessed. She
had chosen two. The first was the most special to Jame-

son. She heard the music fade into the sounding of horns and a voice begin to address the crowd.

"Ladies and gentlemen, The President of the United States, Candace Reid and First Lady Jameson Reid."

"I can't wait to see what you picked," Candace said as they walked out onto the stage.

Hail to the Chief echoed through the hall. Candace and Jameson waved to the assembled crowd and acknowledged the performers before taking their place center stage. Candace kept hold of Jameson's hand as she stepped to the microphone.

"Thank you." She repeated her thanks several times until the room settled. "Thank you all," she said. "I'm so happy to see all of you. I know many of you braved the cold this morning, and you deserve an evening of warmth and celebration," she said.

"We love you!"

"I love you too," Candace promised. Enthusiastic cheers erupted again. "Jameson and I have ten of these wonderful Inaugural Balls to attend. We wanted to start here. This Diversity Ball reflects so many of the reasons I ran my campaign. It reflects who America is. Look around you at the sea of color. Everyone choosing a gown or a tuxedo that reflects their personality. Diversity is everywhere. I still think that's what makes life interesting; all that color." She stopped and took a breath. "I'm standing here because of all of you. Because of your love and support, your hard work and dedication, and believe me; I know it, and I will never forget it. I want to take a minute and acknowledge our family. Most of you will recognize their faces over there. We wouldn't be here without their constant love and support. Like this country, our family continues to grow. We just learned we'll be welcoming another grandchild this year. Just another reason for us all to celebrate tonight." Congratulatory shouts were called out. "Thank you." Candace took a breath. "I know that Jameson has a few things to say — if you can get past how fabulous she looks and listen." Laughter and applause filled the hall. Candace stepped aside to give Jameson the mic.

Jameson laughed. "Trust me; Candace can make anyone look good," she said.

More delighted laughter filtered everywhere.

"Candace mentioned our family. We are blessed with amazing parents and compassionate children. It keeps us on our toes. It also keeps us grounded. Candace knows why she's standing here. I can't tell you how much I appreciate your love and support for her and our family. You should know, she started working the moment she stepped off that platform today." Jameson paused. She'd prepared remarks, but those words did not seem to resonate now. She decided to speak her heart. "What none of you know is that she has no idea what song the band is about to play."

The audience laughed.

"Not everyone gets to surprise the president."
Jameson looked at Candace and then back to the
crowd. "I think the song speaks to more than how
much I love her. It reflects how much you love her too.
And, while I may be biased," Jameson offered a glance
to the band. She looked at Candace and smiled. "I
think we've all been searching for someone exactly like
you."

On cue the band started to play a familiar Van
Morrison tune; one that Jameson had often played in
the background while she and Candace sat in front of
the fireplace dining on chicken wings and wonton
soup. She turned and pulled Candace close.

Candace shook her head and smiled as Jameson
turned her on the dance floor. She could hear the applause in the background. Nothing at the moment mattered to her except Jameson and the lyrics that carried
to her ears. She loved to dance with Jameson.

Jameson's cheek pressed to Candace's as they
swayed together on the stage. "I love you."

Candace breathed Jameson in. She pulled back
slightly to look at Jameson. Her eyes sparkled with
love and admiration. She couldn't recall a president
kissing his wife on the dance floor. She grinned mis-
chievously. She wasn't a *he*. Candace often thought the
world could stand to see more kissing and less killing.
Her hand reached for Jameson's cheek. "I love you
too," she promised. Her lips met Jameson's softly in a
tentative yet loving kiss.

"Holy shit!" Michelle started to laugh. "Can't say I recall seeing that before."

"I think people had better start expecting the unexpected," Marianne commented.

"Safe bet," Pearl chimed.

The hall filled with the sound of whistles and whoops.

Candace giggled. She wiped a familiar smudge of red from the corner of Jameson's mouth.

"I can't believe you did that," Jameson whispered.

"A little more kissing in this world couldn't hurt."

"I'll remember you said that when we get home."

"I'm sure you will," Candace said as the music finished. She waved to the hall again. She turned and waved to their family.

Cooper's eyes were pleading. Candace beckoned him over. He sprinted for his parents. The band played an upbeat tune and Jameson lifted Cooper. Candace kissed his cheek, leaving a smudge. Jameson set him back down and Candace began to dance with him.

The crowd offered its approval.

"You weren't kidding," Michelle said to Marianne. "They're nuts," she laughed.

Jameson couldn't stop herself, she laughed.

"Is my dancing that bad?" Candace asked.

Jameson took Cooper's other hand and leaned into Candace's ear. "No, I was just thinking there is no one better to run the greatest asylum on earth."

"Lunatic," Candace said.

"First Lunatic, Madame President."

"No," Cooper said. "She's just Mommy."

Candace laughed. She bent down and kissed Cooper. "That's exactly right, Cooper." She looked back at Jameson. "Don't ever let me forget that."

"You won't," Jameson said.

The pair turned with Cooper between them and waved goodbye.

"Mommy?"

"Yes, sweetheart?"

"Can I go with you and Momma?"

Candace looked at Jameson. Jameson shrugged. "You can go to one more," Candace said.

"With you?"

Candace nodded. "With us."

Jameson laughed. "Sucker," she whispered.

"I promised my presidency would be about family. Seems like a good way to start."

"Tongues will be wagging later," Jameson said as they stepped backstage.

Candace stopped, kissed Jameson gently and let her lips hover next to Jameson's ear. "I certainly hope so."

Jameson swallowed hard. She laughed when Candace winked at her. "All Hail the Chief," she said.

Candace joined in the laughter. "Don't you forget it."

The End

To Be Continued In
SITUATION ROOM

Made in the USA
Monee, IL
28 July 2023

40051963R00154